A Broken Child Saved by God's Grace

Silence Can Destroy You!

by Sheila Dorsey

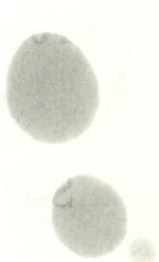

Email: sdorsey1969@aol.com

Cover Design: CTS Graphic Designs

Interior Editor: Margaret Diehl

ISBN: 978-0-692-11546-6

Dedication

≈

This book is dedicated to God (who saved a wretch like me), my kids (Anthony Davis II, Britney Davis, Nastassja Long, Taja Dorsey, and Mysheka Brown), and best friend (Marcia Green) who encouraged me to write and keep writing. This book is also dedicated to the Tinas of the world and in some cases Tims. I love Jesus Christ because he died for my sins and simply because He heard my cries. I pray that this book will be your voice and let you know that you too can get through whatever life throws at you, through prayer. You too can set goals and achieve them despite your past circumstances. Remember with God, all things are possible! Your past does not define your destiny. Also, know that your plans are not always God's plans. His plans for you are far better than you can imagine. Finally, this book is dedicated to freedom. To God, be the glory!

"If you declare with your mouth, 'Jesus is Lord,' and believe in your heart that God raised him from the dead, you will be saved" (New International Version, Rom. 10.9).

"For God so loved the world, that he gave his only begotten Son, that whosoever believeth in him should not perish, but have everlasting life" (King James Version, Jhn. 3.16).

Contents

≈

Preface

≈

This book was written because at around 2:30 AM one morning, after a bout of insomnia, the thought to write a book just mysteriously popped into my head. I believed it was God who put that thought there. Just as quick as the thought appeared, I began to talk out loud to myself and to God, saying, "I don't have time for that. I have my shows to watch on TV, and I hate writing." I pretty much talked myself out of it. Keep in mind, I was not working and had all the time in the world but just didn't see myself doing that. Also, my mom had passed away, so I was no longer helping to take care of her. The very next day I was talking to one of my daughters (as we normally do on the phone), and out of the blue she said, "Ma, you should write a book." I was in such shock that I had to share with her what had happened the day before. That was my confirmation and all I could do was say, "God, I hear you." I started writing at the end of January 2018 and finished at the end of March 2018. This is the finished product.

Introduction

≈

A broken little girl named Tina Robinson lived in Phoenix, Arizona, with her parents, Luke (her stepfather) and Nashay (her mother) Robinson, as well as with her four half-brothers (Darrius, Hakeem, Vince, and Liam). Tina's stepfather was the only father she'd known, since her real father (Vance Days, aka Lifeline) was serving a life sentence in prison for murder. Her mom had Tina's last name changed from Days to Robinson once her real father was completely out of the picture. They lived in a beautiful two-story, five-bedroom, three-bathroom home. Tina's parents were not affectionate people, which is how they were raised by their own parents. She and her siblings never heard I love you, you're beautiful/handsome, and/or you're smart from their parents like other children did. Also, she and her siblings grew up in a non-denominational church. Tina was baptized around the age of ten, which started her on a journey to healing, forgiveness, and self-understanding. She had accepted Jesus Christ in her life/heart as her own personal Savior. She began to build a relationship with God and soon would have to call on Him for strength, endurance, and to keep her sanity.

Tina's brokenness began when she was eight years old. Between the ages of eight and thirteen, she was abused many times. The abuse not only broke her heart but her spirit. She could not understand why those horrible things were happening to her, being that she was only a child. She began to think that her overly developed, adult-looking body was indeed a curse. She began to distrust most of her male family members because she feared that eventually another of them, in a devilish state of mind, would try to touch her inappropriately. She grew to hate them with a passion. Tina truly thought that she would lose her mind before she reached adulthood.

Throughout life, by the grace of God, Tina learned to forgive, love herself more, know her worth, love others, and trust again. Because she learned those things, God's grace (which changed her from the inside out) could guide her to her ordained destiny. That meant that no one or nothing could stop it or take it away from her, because it was God's will. Life for Tina was not easy, but it sculpted her into the woman she was today.

"For I know the plans I have for you," declares the Lord, "plans to prosper you and not to harm you, plans to give you hope and a future" (New International Version, Jer. 29.11).

Chapter 1 - Brokenness

≈

Tina Robinson couldn't remember many good things about her childhood before the tender age of eight. She dwelled in a self-induced fog of forgetfulness. She had experienced abuse by six different male family members over a six-year period. Not only did Tina not trust her male relatives, she had begun to not trust anyone. She felt that even though she had said nothing about the abuse, someone should have known that something was wrong by the change in her behavior and perhaps her appearance. Maybe to them, her behavior was imperceptible, which was why they didn't pick up on the way she was acting out. Tina had sucked her two middle fingers on her right hand since birth; after what she went through, she picked up the habit of twirling her hair while she sucked her fingers. That too became her way of coping with her feelings. That was her security blanket in the privacy of her own room.

Tina's first abuse happened the last time she (at eight years old) visited her grandma Pearl Henderson (maternal grandmother). Her grandad Jimmy Henderson (maternal granddad) was never around and was considered a rolling stone, as he had many girlfriends. Every summer, she and her siblings would go to visit their grandparents for two weeks. They lived about two hours away. Tina and her siblings loved spending time over there. They would all play games and eat good soul food. Out of all her aunts and uncles, Tina had one favorite uncle named Triston Henderson, who was twenty years old. He was a musician and played the saxophone for a local club. He was

1

considered the fun uncle because he was the one who would come up with all the amazing games that she and her siblings played.

One Saturday, Grandma took her grandsons to the grocery store to get food to cook for dinner. Tina stayed home with her favorite uncle. They were home alone, sitting in the family room watching a TV show called *Creature Features*. Her uncle wanted to play a game, and she was so excited that she couldn't contain herself. He went into his bedroom and instructed her to come along. He was wearing dark blue jeans, with a red Adidas shirt and socks. Tina was wearing light blue jeans, with a shiny white blouse and white flip flops. Uncle Triston lay on his full-size bed and told her to come and lie down beside him. She had been brought up to respect her elders and do what they said. Her uncle then began to grab her hands and guide them toward his zipper, to assist him in zipping down his pants. Once his pants were unzipped, his penis began to expand outside of his jeans. Tina soon found out that her uncle wasn't wearing any underwear. The game that they were to play turned out to be Tina fondling her uncle's penis. He knew that this game had to be a quick one because everyone would be back home soon from the grocery store. He proceeded to take her hands yet again and guide them toward his private parts. With his hands placed on top of hers, he continued to stroke them up and down on his shaft until he relieved himself of the pressure that had built up inside. A whitish fluid erupted all over the place. There was a distinct musky smell coming from his genitalia. That smell was now on her hands and in her nostrils. No matter what she did or how hard she tried, she could not wash that smell off her hands or get it out of her nostrils. He cleaned himself up, zipped up his pants, and they both went back into the family room to finish watching TV. Tina was astonished at what had just taken place. It felt like she was in a dream or the Twilight Zone.

Grandma and Tina's siblings returned home from the grocery store and carried all the groceries into the house. No one noticed anything, and she and her uncle carried on as if nothing had happened. A couple of things did happen though. Tina no longer considered him to be her favorite uncle, and she no longer trusted him. She was so ready to go back home to her parents' house, but she had to wait two more days for her summer vacation to be over. She didn't participate in any more games that were played during those last two days at her grandma's house. Tina and her siblings returned home to their parents, and she never visited her grandma's house again. Her parents didn't even question her as to why she never wanted to go back to her grandma's house for the summer. They just figured that she had caught an attitude with her grandma because Grandma wouldn't let her have her way. Tina was a bit traumatized by her uncle's game and never spoke of that event.

Tina's second disaster occurred one day when she was nine years old, at home doing her chores. She was washing the dishes and wiping down the countertops. She was wearing loose fitting, mid-thigh, navy blue shorts, a gray tank top, and no shoes. Her uncle (on her mother's side) named Chris Henderson, twenty-three years old, often came by to visit her mother. He was wearing an all-black sweat suit, black Timberland boots, and a black Kangol hat. No one liked him because of his ruthless reputation. He weighed around two hundred and fifty pounds and stood around six feet tall. He had a muscular build, a result of his workout regime when he was last in prison. He was a street thug and was known to be in a notorious street gang called the Phoenix Thug Lords. That gang was known for drug dealing/trafficking, robbing people, beating up people, and in some cases, killing people. So whenever he came around, most of her family was terrified. Even though her family was scared, they did everything in their power to not show their fear. They never knew when someone from a rival gang was going to retaliate against her uncle and possibly come after his family.

Tina's brothers were outside playing, and her mom was in the bedroom sleeping when her uncle came into the kitchen and began a casual conversation with her. While she was wiping down the countertops, he came up behind her and began to aggressively grind on her butt with his body/private area. He began to grope her butt with his hands as if he were trying to have sex with her in somewhat of a doggy-style position. Tina tried to quickly move away from him, but she was trapped between the cabinet and his strong grip and could not move. She began to cough/slightly choke from the cheap cologne he was wearing. Once she caught her breath, she began to talk very loudly in hopes that her mom would hear her and wake up. She was telling her uncle to stop and that if he didn't, she would tell her mother and stepfather what he was doing to her. She knew he was high on drugs, because along with the cheap cologne smell, he reeked of marijuana, and she assumed that was why he was acting like a savage. He finally stopped what he was doing to her and rushed out of the front door. Tina didn't say anything to anyone about that ordeal. She just kept it to herself. Her uncle did continue to come around now and then, but he never touched her again. She believed that he had come to his senses and realized that he was totally wrong that day.

Tina's third calamity transpired when, at ten years old, she went over to her twenty-five-year-old paternal cousin's house to borrow a cup of sugar for her mom. She was wearing pink pants and a pink tank top, with pink sneakers. His house was literally across the street from her

4

house. Her mom would always send her over to her cousin's house to borrow eggs, sugar, milk, or whatever she needed to cook if she didn't have it in the house. Her mom didn't want to make a trip to the grocery store in the middle of cooking dinner. There were times when she would send one of Tina's brothers over to borrow the item, but they were usually outside somewhere playing, just being boys, out of sight until the sun went down. That left Tina at her mother's beck and call.

Her cousin, Randell Lovely, who was a middle school math teacher, was a nice person, but he had a dark side. One Tuesday evening, Tina would find out what that dark side was. She knocked on her cousin's door, and he answered. He was wearing white-washed blue jeans, with no shirt or socks, and was home alone. He had broad shoulders and was very muscular. She said to him, "My mom wants to borrow a cup of sugar" as she handed him an empty plastic Tupperware container with a lid.

He said, "Sure, come on in." He then said, "Follow me to the kitchen." He filled the container up with sugar, put the lid back on it tight, and handed it back to her. As she turned around to walk toward the door, he ran up behind her and attempted to pull her pants down. Tina was not sure of what would have happened to her had he succeeded in pulling her pants down, but she was not going to stick around to find out. She ran toward the door holding the container full of sugar with one hand and holding on to her pants with the other. It was a struggle, but she managed to get out of the door with her pants still on/up. She then ran all the way home. Tina, once again, did not mention what had happened to her to anyone. Whenever her mom needed to borrow something else from her cousin's house, Tina would find one of her brothers to go over there instead. In her mind, that was best, because her cousin wasn't interested in little boys; he was interested in little girls.

Tina's fourth heartbreak took place when she was eleven years old. She and her cousin Chester Redmond (on her real father's side of the family) used to hang out with each other all the time. They were not best friends but were very close. They would hang out in Tina's front yard, laughing and having fun. Chester was sixteen years old, had no intentions of ever working, hated school but loved sports. He believed that the many girls that he was dating all at the same time should always take care of him, be it physically or financially. He thought that he was the ladies' man. He was already six feet two, had a slim build and was very light-skinned, with good hair. He also had the perfect white teeth and smile. Apparently, the girls whom he was charming thought that he was very handsome. To Tina, he was just her ugly, big-headed cousin.

Her cousin came over after school one day in his basketball uniform because he had just finished basketball practice. They sat on the bench in Tina's front yard, watching the cars go by. They were gossiping about the neighbors who made them laugh. Also, they talked about their dreams, goals, and ambitions. That day her cousin decided to cross the line of cousinship. Normally, he would always greet her with a brief hug. On that day, she noticed that he hugged her a little longer, was more touchy-feely, and ended up kissing her on her neck. She thought all that to be very weird, and it was certainly uninvited. He decided to ask her to have sex with him. She said to him, "Dude, no way!" She also said to him, "You do know that we are cousins, right?"

He said to her, "I know, but if you will not have sex with me, then maybe I could perform oral sex on you. No one would have to know." She was thinking, no not you too! Tina told her cousin never to ask those type of questions or speak to her again in that manner. He agreed and walked away. He looked back at her with a big smile, licked his lips and said, "If you ever change your mind, let me know." Because that was such an awkward moment for her, they never again hung out like they used to. She didn't look at him the same after that.

Tina's mom shared with her a rumor that she believed. It was rumored that Chester's mom slept with Tina's stepfather and her stepfather's father, but it was never confirmed or proven. If it were true, that would make Chester Tina's stepbrother or uncle. Either way, she felt a brotherly connection with him. She kept her guard up whenever he was around because of what had happened earlier. He was somewhat of a protector of her, keeping the bad guys from talking to or trying to hurt her.

Tina's fifth and worst catastrophe ensued when she was at twelve years old. She was at home, sleeping in her twin bed one night, and awoke to a bright light shining on her face. She lifted her head to see where the light was coming from and realized it was coming from her parents' room. Their room was diagonally across the hall from hers. That night, her mother was not home because she worked the graveyard shift in the morgue, at a local hospital. Her stepfather was a sheriff and worked during the day. When she raised her head up to look toward the bright light, she made eye contact with her stepfather. He told her, "Come here." Judging by the tone of his voice, Tina felt deep down inside that something wasn't right. But, as she was told, she got up and walked into the room where her stepfather was sitting on the edge of their king-size bed, in his black pajamas. As she got closer to the bed, he could see the frightened look on her face, which should have scared him too, but did not. Tina was wearing her favorite light-blue nightgown, which had big navy-blue stars on the front of it, over her chest area. Her gown covered her fully, from her neck down to her ankles. She was trying to figure out why would he ask her to come into their room so late at night? She knew that she hadn't done anything wrong and shouldn't be in any kind of trouble. She was just standing there, looking scared and confused. She then glanced over at the TV and saw that there were a naked man and women exercising on the TV screen. She wondered what kind of show was he watching. Without saying another word, her stepfather lifted her gown up to her waist area, pulled the elastic at the top of her panties away from her body, and looked down into her panties toward her private area. He stared at her private area for around two minutes, but to Tina, it felt like a lifetime. She stared at the wall in front of her as if she were in a trance. Her stepfather then let go of her panties, and her gown dropped back to her ankles. He said, "Don't say anything to anybody because I don't want to get into trouble."

Tina couldn't believe what had just happened. She was wondering exactly what he was looking for. Was he checking to see if she had a hygiene problem, if she had pubic hairs, or if her period was on at that exact moment? She had started her period when she was nine years old. She was in total shock and didn't know what to do or think. She wanted her mom so badly, but she wasn't there. She even blamed her mom because she felt that if her mom were home doing her wifely duties, this would have never happened. Also, she low-key condemned her real father for not being there to protect her. Her brothers were in their rooms sleeping. Tina turned around and walked back to her room with tears running down her face as she began to pray.

She was so devastated. It shook her to the core. Her heart was broken; her mind was destroyed, and her trust for her stepfather died that night. She became very fragile and demoralized. For Tina, things were never the same in the

Robinson family household. She did not breathe a word of what had happened to her to anyone. She had made up her mind that she would carry this secret to her grave. She didn't want her stepfather to go to prison or to break apart their family. She didn't want her family, friends, or other people to look at her stepfather in a bad way or differently. However, she did begin to pray more and sleep with a bible and a kitchen knife under her pillow. In her mind, those three things were her protection now. She had no one to turn to but God.

After that night, her stepfather began to come to her bedroom door to see if she was awake. Tina would shut her eyes as tight as she could, pretending that she was asleep. He would begin to whistle loudly enough to wake her up – if she had been asleep – but quietly enough that he wouldn't wake up her brothers. After a few nights of doing that and not being able to get her to open her eyes, he finally left her alone and never tried anything with her again. She was so happy about that, but she continued praying and sleeping with a bible and a kitchen knife under her pillow, just in case. Although she didn't tell her mother what had happened to her that night, she did ask her, "Why is Dad coming to my bedroom door at night and whistling as if he is trying to wake me up?"

Her mom said, "He's just checking on you and your brothers when I'm at work." Her stepfather did go to her brothers' room and look in on them, but he didn't whistle at them trying to wake them up as he had done to her. Tina wanted to tell her mom that what she was saying wasn't true, but she let it be. She didn't want to hurt anyone or be the cause of their family breaking up.

That whole incident caused a great rift between Tina and her stepfather. She began to really act out and talk back to her parents, even though she would get smacked in the mouth. She was trying to figure out why was this happening to her. He was the only father she'd known, for goodness sake. He was supposed to love her and protect her. She was supposed to be able to always trust him. She was supposed to be Daddy's little girl. Instead, she began to hate him for doing that to her. Also, she felt that her mother should have sensed that something was off in their household. She believed that her mom wasn't using her motherly intuition.

Tina's sixth misfortune occurred when she, at thirteen years old, was outside with her best friends and younger cousins playing hide-go-seek. Her eighteen-year-old paternal cousin, Jersey Brown, was watching from inside his home as she ran around in her little red short shorts. He was wearing blue jeans with a plain white T-shirt. He saw her hiding spot and decided to startle her by rushing up behind her and grabbing her butt. She screamed and ran down the street to where her paternal aunt (Reba Days) was standing and told her what had just happened. Her aunt said to her, "Why are you lying?"

If looks could kill, her aunt would have been dead from the look that Tina gave her. Tina walked away in such shock and anger that her aunt didn't believe her, she vowed never to mention again that her cousin had grabbed her butt.

Two months later, Tina's parents signed her up for cheerleading. She was on a little league team called the Phoenix Red Hawks. One weekday after cheerleading practice, she ran into her cousin again. Her aunt must have told him what Tina had said about grabbing her butt because he asked her, "Why did you tell your aunt what happened?"

She replied, "I don't know."

He was wearing a red polo shirt with khaki pants. He was at the field because he was the coach for one of the Little League football teams. That same cousin that two months earlier grabbed her butt was beginning to spin his web of deceit. He persuaded her to sit in his car for a little while, to listen to the music that was playing on the radio. He offered her some snacks (candy, potato chips, and a coke), and that seemed to do the trick. Once Tina's cousin got her all comfortable and relaxed in his car, swaying to the music and eating snacks, he then made his next move. He reclined her seat back a little. He started by rubbing his hand on her inner thigh just to see how she would react or if she would scream as she had before when he grabbed her butt. She didn't say anything but froze up a little. He eventually moved his hand under her cheerleading skirt, heading directly to the front of her bloomers. He wasted no time at getting to what he wanted. He proceeded to pull her bloomers over to one side, exposing her private area. That gave him access to her vagina. He began to slide his middle finger inside of her vagina as he grabbed and rubbed his crotch. She looked at him kind of weird, but she didn't tell him to stop or attempt to move his hand away. Then he took his finger back out. She was wondering, why did he do that and exactly what was he feeling for? Tina was in shock and wanted help, but she remembered that her aunt did not believe her when she told her that her cousin had grabbed her butt. Because of that, she felt that no one would believe her if she told or even if she screamed. No one would ever believe her, regardless.

He smoothly glided his middle finger inside of her again, let it rest there for a little while, and then took it back out. She sat and watched him smell and lick his middle finger. They said their goodbyes. After that, Tina walked over to the front of the practice field's office where her brothers were standing so that she wouldn't miss her ride home with her parents. She never spoke of that moment or saw her cousin again until later.

Tina's parents wanted to spice up their marriage by going out on date nights. They decided that at least twice a month, they would go out to the movies, dinner, dancing, etc. That would have to take place on a weekend, when they both were off at the same time and their schedules didn't conflict. That sounded like a perfect plan at first, but there was one small problem. They didn't have anyone to watch their kids. Tina's stepfather must have run into her cousin Jersey down the street because the next thing she knew, he walked into their house, saying to her mom that he'd be there Saturday to watch the kids. Saturday came around, and he was there on time. Tina thought that if her parents trusted him to babysit them, he must be an alright guy after all. She began to look at him as a knight in shining armor who would rescue her from the fire-breathing dragon who was her stepfather. She now had a man who would love her and protect her, someone she was starting to really trust after all that had happened to her thus far. Everything went like clockwork. Every other weekend, her cousin would be there ready to babysit. When her parents went on their date, her cousin made sure that she and her siblings completed any homework that needed to be done, ate dinner, took a bath, and went to bed by a certain time.

About a month later, Tina's best friend, Rhonda Berry, stayed over one Saturday night. She was thirteen years old as well. That night the kids stayed up late, watched TV and played games. Her brothers fell asleep early. Tina and her best friend were playing a game on the floor in her room when her cousin walked in to play with them. The next thing they knew, the room light was being turned off and the game turned into him touching all over them. They didn't mind because the game seemed kind of fun and mysterious. A few minutes later, he picked her best friend up in his arms and placed her on Tina's twin bed, took off her shorts and panties, dropped them on the floor, unzipped his pants, pulled out his penis, got on top of her, and slid his penis into her vagina. He targeted her because he knew she wasn't a virgin. He knew that she had been violated by one of her male relatives a few years prior and could handle him inside of her. While he was playing a game with her best friend, he instructed Tina to lie on the floor right next to her own bed. With his free hand, he pulled her shorts and panties to the side, stuck his middle finger inside of her vagina vigorously, which cause her to gyrate aggressively to every beat of his finger movement. The three of them were playing this game for about thirty minutes. Tina could hear her cousin hitting the walls of her best friend's vagina with every pump he made. From the floor she could see and feel the bed rocking. She could hear her cousin moaning in pure enjoyment. Right before he reached his peak, he quickly jumped up off Rhonda and ejaculated into a towel that he had put next to them on the bed. Around that same time, Tina became very moist between her legs. She didn't comprehend that she had just had her first orgasm. Tina and Rhonda were unaware that what they had just experienced was known as a threesome. Her cousin got a kick out of "having his cake and eating it too." Her cousin made sure that when the game was over, she and her best friend cleaned themselves up from the ordeal and were in bed before Tina's parents returned home. Once the parents returned, her cousin left and didn't come back until the next time they needed him to watch their kids. Her best friend went home the next morning because she had to go to church. Neither one of them said a word about what happened that night before. Each time her cousin watched the kids after that, he would wait until her brothers fell asleep and constantly rub on Tina's butt, thighs, and breast. She began to really like the way he was making her feel.

One night, Tina's mother didn't feel like cooking dinner before they went out for their date night and was going to buy her and her siblings some fast food from McDonald's. Her cousin mentioned that he would go get the food for them. He also mentioned that it would be a good idea for Tina to go with him, just to make sure that he got the order right and to help hold the food in the car. On the way to McDonald's, her cousin drove off the main road and onto a dark, deserted road, where there was little to no traffic. He parked the car on the side of the road, in an open patch of grass. It was obvious that he had been there before because he knew exactly where to go, as if he had already had something planned. He turned off the car, which made it pitch black. He instructed her to get into the back seat of the car, which she did with no hesitation. He proceeded to follow her into the back seat. Then he began to touch her body all over. While touching her, he managed to ease her shorts and panties off and sat them neatly on the floor of the car. He wanted to make this a pleasant experience for her. He unzipped his pants, took out his penis and gently attempted to slide it into Tina's vagina. Her eyes grew big because of what she felt down there, when his shaft touched the opening of her vagina. She could tell that he was rather large. It took him several tries because she was still a virgin, but he finally succeeded at pushing through. She wasn't sure what or how to feel, but she was in a lot of pain and it felt good at the same time. She knew by his reaction (moans and gyrations) that this was something he was really enjoying. That was the defining moment when she equated sex with love. When he felt that he was going to explode, he removed himself quickly from her vagina and ejaculated on an old dirty beach towel that he had in his car. When he was all done cleaning himself and Tina up, he zipped his pants back up, and she put her panties and shorts back on. They got back into the front seats of the car and

14

made sure they both looked the same as when they left her parents' house, and nothing was out of place. He cranked up his car and headed to McDonald's to get the food, acting as if nothing had happened. When they returned to Tina's house with the food, she was hoping that her parents wouldn't notice that her walk was different, and they didn't. That was the night that her cousin took her virginity, and she couldn't get him off her mind. She had fallen in love with him. He was her first love, a forbidden love.

Her cousin continued to babysit several times after that night, and they would touch, grind, and kiss each other. He knew that she loved him even though they were only together in that way that one time. He was in love with her too, she believed. One night while they were both attending a high school football game, he took up for her. He stopped guys from trying to talk to her and flirt with her. She was very cold, so he gave her his jacket to wear. An older high school boy came up to talk to her, grabbing the jacket she was wearing, and her cousin just lost it. He quickly jacked the high school boy up in the air (off his feet) and threw him down to the ground. His actions and body language expressed to that guy to back off her and that she belonged to him. He didn't need to utter a single word. She loved that feeling of being protected and longed to be with him sexually again, but again never came.

Shortly after that incident, she was told by her stepfather that she couldn't be around him and that he couldn't be around her anymore. She wasn't sure what went wrong. She wondered who was going to protect and love her now? Who was she going to trust? After all, she felt that he had saved her from her stepfather possibly being the one who took her virginity. Just like that, he was no longer her or her siblings' babysitter. The next time she saw her cousin was when she was an adult. In a sick and twisted kind of way, her heart was crushed that she

15

couldn't see or be around her cousin anymore. She didn't quite understand that what she and her cousin had done was morally wrong and was considered incest.

Over time, Tina recovered and realized that her cousin was an adult and knew better. He chose to take advantage of her. She soon realized that her cousin didn't really love her but only wanted to be the first to get what was between her legs. He probably just wanted to add this to his trophy case so to speak. Tina knew there had to be others. She understood that this tainted love was full of lies and deceit and that this forbidden love could never be. She also recognized that he had been prepping, grooming, and preparing her all this time, just to take her virginity. With all the grown women in the world, he chose to prey on her, a young teen. Not to mention he had a girlfriend that Tina knew nothing about until everything was over. She began to hear rumors about what she and her cousin had done. She felt very ashamed and embarrassed that she had allowed this to happen to her. She asked God repeatedly to forgive her sins. She also heard rumors that her cousin finagled his way out of being beaten to a pulp by her stepfather and facing charges of statutory rape for taking her innocence.

She began to look at her life thus far and could not understand why those things with her male family members had happened to her. At times, she would be angry with God and blame Him for allowing all of that to happen. Out of all the abusive events that she endured, the one that broke her the most mentally, emotionally, and spiritually, was the encounter she had had with her stepfather. He was supposed to be her protector. None of her male relatives ever came to her and apologized for what they had done. It no longer mattered anyway because the damage (mentally, emotionally, physically, and spiritually) was already done.

Because of it, she pretty much became a loner and only had a few friends.

Tina's brokenness was bound to lead her into an early journey to single motherhood. She saw and was exposed to too much, too early in life, when most kids were just playing and being kids. Her young mind and body were already thrust into adulthood. She had no choice at that point but to deal with the cards that she was dealt. So, she did what she knew. She survived (mentally, emotionally, physically, etc.) the best way she knew how.

"Trust in the Lord with all thine heart; and lean not unto thine own understanding. In all thy ways acknowledge him, and he shall direct thy paths" (King James Version, Prov. 3.5-6).

Trust

Trust, where are you? I seek you, yet I cannot find you. We went our separate ways early in this life.

Trust, are you not earned? Some trust until a reason is given for them not to. I must be given a reason to and/or shown that I can trust.

Trust, I've reached out to you, but you did not grab my hand. Trust, I've longed for you, but you did not understand. Trust, I've prayed for you, and God is on His way.

Trust, I love you, I want you, I need you, and I am willing to try, for you. Please, just give me a chance.

Chapter 2 - Journey to Single Motherhood

≈

Tina no longer had the comfort of her cousin's arms nor did she have the love and protection of her stepfather. She didn't want it either. She just couldn't trust them anymore. Tina had learned to associate sex with love. Because of this, she began to look for what she thought was love – in all the wrong places. She was lost yet trying to be found. She was blind and trying to see through a cloudy and damaged lens. If a guy told her that she was fine, looked good, was beautiful or cute, she slept with him. If a guy showed her any attention or affection, she gave him the goods. If a guy said that he liked her, loved her, or wanted to get to know her, he could get it easily. Tina's finger-sucking and hair-twirling continued from this point and would eventually carry into her adulthood. Whenever she got serious with a guy, she would tell him about her habits, and this was usually received well and loved. In some cases, it would turn into a form of foreplay. She felt that, eventually, one of those sexual relationships would turn into a real loving relationship. The kind of relationship that she could one day take home to mama, so to speak. Because of her way of thinking, Tina ended up having a total of five children out of wedlock before she reached the age of twenty-six. The children were from five different boys/men. She gave birth to one daughter, three sons, and lost a child she never knew.

Tina first found herself pregnant at the tender age of thirteen. She was scared and didn't know what she was going to do. She did not want to have kids at an early age.

She wanted to grow up, start a career, get married, and then have kids, in that exact order. She knew her baby father (Leonard High) before getting pregnant because his sister (Belinda High) was one of her best friends. He was a seventeen-year-old high school senior with plans to go off to college shortly after graduation. He was five feet eleven and had a dark brown-sugar complexion. Tina thought he was fine.

One day during the school week, Tina and her best friend decided to skip school and hang out at her best friend's house. Leonard and his friends were also hanging out there. They were all high school seniors and participated in senior skip day. There were no adults on site to supervise any mischievous behavior that might occur. Tina had a huge crush on Leonard. She noticed that he was wearing some army green shorts that came down to his knees, a tan T-shirt, and tan shoes. He was nicely groomed. He paid her no mind at first because she was just his little sister's very young best friend. Then she began to flirt with him a little. He responded to her flirting with a little flirting of his own. That flirting soon became a game of playing doctor. He was the doctor, and Tina was the patient. The game started in her best friend's room. Leonard was to give her a checkup/physical. She stood against the wall for him to begin. He first checked her chest, which was to get a quick feel of her breast. Then he checked her backside to see if there were any superfluous lumps apparent, which translated into a quick feel of her butt. After that, he checked her lips, which was a chance to sneak a very long, lovely French kiss. That kiss landed them inside of his bedroom. He closed his room door and locked it for privacy. His full-size bed was not made up, and he had white cotton sheets. Tina became very nervous at that point. She was wondering, does he really like me? She thought he must like her because he was showing interest.

Tina was wearing tan short shorts, a red shirt, and black sandals. She and Leonard lay down on his bed staring at each other while rubbing on each other's arms. He then unzipped his shorts, and she unzipped hers. They kissed again, and when she finally caught her breath, her shorts and panties were on the floor next to the bed and so were his. He had to have taken them off because she didn't. He must have known a magic trick. Oh, there was magic in his room that day for sure because he took his time with Tina and made her feel like she was the only girl in the world. His final procedure that he had to perform on her, as her doctor, was to check her vagina. He did so by placing his medical instrument into her first aid kit. That procedure lasted for a while until his lubricant was about to seep out into her. Leonard was her first time having relations because the encounter that she had with her cousin didn't count, because she wished it didn't happen.

Leonard then rose up out of Tina's first aid kit so that he wouldn't leave anything behind, but he wasn't quite successful. Tina was so naive that she thought that because she saw some of his lubricant on the bed, she was safe from any repercussions. Perhaps that was because her parents never had the sex talk with her (most black parents didn't). She wasn't on birth control. She didn't comprehend that it would only take just one drop of his lubricant to change her life forever.

Neither Tina nor Leonard were worried. They both put their underwear and shorts back on because his friends were banging on his locked bedroom door. Her best friend was outside of the house, standing at her brother's room window, trying to see what was going on while laughing aloud. Once they were dressed, Leonard unlocked his room door and opened it. At that point, all his friends and sister were standing at the door looking around, just trying to be nosey. Despite their age difference, Tina was sure that she and Leonard would become a couple. Boy, was she dead wrong!

After that day, whenever she came over to their house to hang out with his sister, he paid her no attention at all. He acted as if she wasn't even there and said nothing to her. The way he was treating her hurt her feelings badly. She felt used and real low. She walked away from that house that day not knowing the big surprise that was in store for her.

A month later, Tina began to feel sick. She had started having morning sickness/nausea, sore nipples, she slept a lot, and she ate a lot. She also missed her menstrual cycle that month. Those were all telltale signs that Tina was indeed pregnant. Tina wasn't sure, so she just kept the possibility of her being pregnant to herself. Soon her stomach began to grow, and her parents became suspicious. Her mother noticed that she had not asked her for any maxi pads, as she normally would every month. Her stepdad noticed that every time that she sat down, she would take a nap, which was not normal for her. Tina could tell that both of her parents knew something was different about her. She was very afraid and didn't know what to do. Again, she still wasn't certain if she, in fact, was pregnant. She didn't know how her parents would react if she told them that she might be pregnant. She didn't want them to kill her, literally.

Tina begin to wear baggy clothing to hide her growing belly. She became a pro at hiding things like when she had to upchuck. She would walk into the family room over to the window, facing the concrete driveway, and open it. Then she would quickly push the screen out onto the concrete driveway, hang her head out of the window, and throw up. That was done to prevent her from regurgitating in the bathroom near her parents' bedroom. She then hurried to walk outside to get the water hose, turned on the

24

water, and rinsed the vomit into the grass. Then she had to return the screen back to its rightful place in the window frame, take the water hose back to its original location, and turn the water off. Tina rushed back into the house and let the window back down, all without her parents' knowledge.

One morning, Tina's mother took Tina on a ride, pretending to take her shopping. Instead, she took her to a place called Acacia Women's Center for a pregnancy test. That place also performed abortions. Tina was very nervous, and her mother had that look – you better not be pregnant – on her face. As far as her mom and stepdad were concerned, she shouldn't have been doing anything unladylike anyway. Tina had denied it every time they asked her, "Are you doing something?"

Once they parked the car and walked inside the center, Tina's mother had to sign her in to be seen by a nurse since she was still a minor. Fifteen minutes later, the nurse called Tina's name to take a pregnancy test. The walk to that back room was the longest walk ever. Her mother took that walk with her. Tina felt like a "dead man walking." She went into the restroom, peed in the cup that she was given, and handed it back to the nurse. She then walked into the little room where her mom and the nurse were sitting and awaited the test results. About five minutes later, Tina was told that her test came back positive. She was so happy that she began to clap her hands in a celebratory fashion because, in her guilelessness, she thought that the test meant that she was positively not pregnant. Her mom quickly burst her bubble and cursed her out, from the examining room all the way to the car. They didn't even discuss an abortion; her mother didn't believe in that. On the ride back home and after hearing more choice words from her mother, Tina was given two days to tell her stepfather that she was pregnant, or her mom would tell.

Tina could not get up the nerve to tell her stepdad, so her mom ended up doing it. It was obvious that her parents were very disappointed, but her stepdad took things to the extreme. He barely talked to Tina anymore, and when he did, it was always in an angry tone. He let it be known that he wasn't helping her with anything other than the usual keeping a roof over her and her siblings' heads and food on the kitchen table. Also, he warned her that if she got pregnant again, she would have to get out of his house. She knew that she was going to be miserable living there up until she delivered her baby. All she could think about was that by the time she'd have the baby, she'd have turned fourteen.

Now it was time for Tina to tell her baby father (Leonard) that she was pregnant. She first told his sister and then told him. He asked, "Are you sure, and is it mine?"

She uttered, "Yes, I'm sure, and it's yours!"

Shortly after that conversation, he graduated from high school, left for college, and never looked back. He left Tina alone to have and raise their baby on her own, with the help of her mother. Tina was very angry with him and wanted to let him know that it was her testimony at the sheriff's department that kept him out of jail, which allowed him to go off to college. Her stepdad tried to have him brought up on statutory rape charges, but Tina told the sheriff that Leonard hadn't forced her. She didn't say anything to him, though, because telling him that wasn't going to keep him with her or help her take care of their baby. Tina did learn one of life's most valuable lessons that day, which was having a baby doesn't keep a man.

During Tina's pregnancy, she experienced occasional cravings for watermelon and strawberries. She dealt with her feet and ankles swelling and as her stomach grew, she became more and more uncomfortable. Her stomach was stretched beyond her timid young frame. Even though her pregnancy was considered high-risk (because of her age and body mass), her baby appeared to be healthy, with a strong heartbeat and much movement. Tina began to stick to her mother like glue. She would later refer to herself as her mom's shadow. Tina and her mom became real close during her pregnancy because Tina was scared, didn't know what to do or what to expect, and she relied heavily on her mom for guidance and support. With her mom and help from the welfare system (Medicaid, food stamps, WIC, and cash assistance), most of the expenses related to Tina's pregnancy and delivery were taken care of.

She did stress to her mom that she would like to continue her education, so her mom placed her in a program called Break the Cycle. That program was geared to help first-time teenage moms learn how to care for their babies and themselves, and how to prevent getting pregnant again while continuing their education. Also, after the teenagers delivered their babies, they could continue to go to school there and bring their babies for three months before going back into the public school system. The teenagers also were given opportunities to speak to other teenagers at local middle schools about their pregnancies and the experience (nightmare) of being young mothers. Tina was ecstatic because she was around other people who were in the same boat that she was in. She was relieved because she hated hearing her peers at her previous school whispering and talking about her behind her back and in some cases, to her face. She was already ashamed and had low self-esteem. Tina met her future best friend (Raven Sparks) at that school. They found that they had a lot of things in common and could relate to each other. Raven, too, was molested at an early age, but at the hands of her father's best friend. They had or made fun, even though they had been and were in the mist of storms. They would often talk about their deadbeat baby fathers, and they leaned on each other to get through very difficult times. They begin to hang out more outside of school. Raven would become Tina's daughter's godmother. Tina became Raven daughter's godmother as well. Raven had a zest for education and read a lot of books. Her zeal for education rubbed off on Tina, but her reading all the time, not so much.

One day at home while Tina was talking to her mom in the kitchen, her water broke all over the kitchen floor. After they both cleaned up the kitchen floor, Tina's mom took her to the hospital (the same hospital where she worked) to deliver her baby. She was terrified and in excruciating pain. After twenty-eight hours of labor, no epidural, an episiotomy, and the help of forceps, she delivered a healthy baby girl (Keyla Robinson) naturally. The baby weighed in at six pounds and thirteen ounces and was sixteen inches long. She was beautiful.

Tina was exhausted but quickly fell in love with her baby once she saw and held her for the first time. She learned to breastfeed her baby girl on the spot. She also changed her first poopy diaper, which was not pleasant. Her mom was by her side the entire time. A few of her relatives came by to visit her while she was in the hospital. They really weren't there to see her but just to be nosey. They wanted to see if her baby girl looked like her or her cousin (Jersey). They believed that her baby (Keyla) was conceived with him. That was untrue. The timeline of when everything transpired didn't add up.

Two days later, Tina was released from the hospital to go home and care for her baby. Now on birth control pills, she received a lot of guidance from her mom, but her mom made sure that she took care of her own baby since she was the one who had lain down and got it. That meant that she had a lot of sleepless night dealing with a crying baby, constant breastfeeding, a sick baby, doctor appointments, etc. She also noticed that her stomach now looked and felt like a raisin. She found out from her doctor during her six-week checkup that because she was so young when she had her baby, her stomach would remain that way even if she'd exercised, but the color might lighten up.

Her mom allowed her to go back to school after her six-week follow up. Her mom worked at night and was her babysitter during the day. Tina was so appreciative of what her mom was doing for her. Even though she was sleep-deprived, she knew she had to keep going. She now not only had to take care of herself and her baby when she got home from school, but she also had to do homework, school projects, etc. Life just got real for her. She went on with life despite her struggles and was only able to do so through prayer.

Tina became pregnant again at the age of fifteen, even though she was using contraception. The father (Hakeem Williams) who she claimed was the baby's father was not really the father. She knew that he wasn't, but she desperately wanted him to be. He was the first man that she loved from the heart after her cousin. She lied to him and told him that he was the baby's father. Hakeem was a high school sophomore and worked part-time as a pizza delivery driver after school. He was Tina's height (five feet six inches tall), skinny, and his skin tone was a mocha shade of chocolate. He looked a little like Denzel Washington. He and she were in a serious relationship and had fallen in love quickly. She was on birth control pills, but they did not like using condoms. They didn't enjoy the way condoms felt. It interfered with their sexual pleasure. They made passionate love many times whenever and wherever they could, but Tina never popped up pregnant.

Hakeem was hanging out with his homeboys one night at a house party and let them talk him into sleeping with a random chick. It's obvious that he was weak-willed because he didn't resist and keep his appendage in his pants. Word got back to Tina the very next day that he had cheated on her, and she became enraged. She was downright livid. Because she was hurt and wanted revenge, she decided to sleep with his cousin (Frank Stone) after school one evening. He was a high school sophomore and sixteen years old as well. He worked part-time at a fast food restaurant after school. He was five feet nine inches tall and looked like Morris Chestnut, with a Godiva chocolate skin tone. Tina knew him from school and around the neighborhood. He already had a steady girlfriend but apparently wanted a taste of something new. He was eager to oblige her on getting even with his cousin because he didn't like his cousin; he thought Hakeem was arrogant. They made a plan to meet up at Frank's uncle's apartment to get busy. Before they got busy on his uncle's couch, they kissed and touched each other wildly. They began to rip each other's clothes off as if they just couldn't wait to have each other's hidden treasures. Tina performed fellatio on Frank, and he returned the favor. He then thrusted his milky way into her welcoming, warm galaxy roughly, and they continued like wild animals. Their animalistic behavior carried on for about thirty minutes, and she allowed him to cascade inside of her. She thought it was okay since she was on the pill and hadn't gotten pregnant thus far from Hakeem. Tina and Frank got dressed, hugged, kissed, and said their goodbyes. They meant nothing to each other and didn't see each other much after that escapade.

Later, Tina began to feel weird. It was how she felt during her first pregnancy. She again experienced nausea, sore nipples, a missed period, etc. She didn't really need a

30

pregnancy test but took one anyway. The test result was as expected, positive. Tina was trying to figure out how she was going to tell her parents, her boyfriend, and his cousin that she was pregnant. She remembered what her stepdad said during her first pregnancy – if she got pregnant again, she would have to get out. That had stayed in the back of her mind. So she decided not to say anything to her parents. She planned to just hide her pregnancy. As far as telling her boyfriend, Hakeem, she didn't have to, because he had already heard the news. He was hurt, disgusted, embarrassed, and angry with Tina. He felt that it was okay for him to cheat, but not her. He felt that she had betrayed him in the worst way, as the guy she cheated with was his cousin. He no longer wanted to be in a relationship with her. Apparently, he couldn't have any children due to a childhood accident that had severely damaged his scrotum. So he knew there was no way that her baby could be his.

After their break up, Tina sent word by one of Frank's homeboys to tell him that she was pregnant with his baby. She wanted to let him know in hopes that he would break up with his girlfriend, just like her boyfriend had broken up with her. Frank didn't want anything to do with her or the baby. Tina learned that it didn't pay to cheat, and she was beginning to feel like a Jezebel. Again, she was left alone to raise a child, with the assistance of her mom and the welfare system.

One morning when Tina was getting ready for school, she was in the bathroom standing in front of the mirror, curling her hair, with her arms up in the air. She had on a tight-fitting dress with a cover-up shirt over it. Normally, when she would wear that outfit, she would have the cover up shirt completely buttoned, but for some reason, she didn't this time. Perhaps she was rushing. Her stepfather walked past the bathroom door, looked at her (focusing mainly on her stomach, which was huge) and told

31

her that she had two weeks to get out of his house. He said, "I knew you were pregnant again because you were eating up everything and sleeping too damn much."

She couldn't say anything because she was, in fact, pregnant again. She knew her stepfather was angry and probably still disappointed in her, but she didn't take his threat seriously. He knew that she didn't have anywhere else to go and that she was still a minor. So she carried on with life as usual. Tina's mom couldn't believe her daughter was pregnant again, but she dealt with it the best way she knew how by supporting her. Tina's mom finally stood up for her. She made a threat of her own and gave her stepdad an ultimatum. She told him that he was not going to put their daughter or their grandchildren out on the streets and if he did, she was leaving with them. He quickly had a change of heart and allowed them to stay in his house. Tina and her stepfather still bumped heads and didn't see eye to eye, so she attempted to stay out of his way as much as possible. It was obvious that the pill did not work for her and after she had the baby, she would need to try a different type of contraception.

During this pregnancy, she craved pineapples and milk. Other than that, her pregnancy wasn't too bad. Tina continued her education up until she went into labor. The just-turned- sixteen-year old's labor started while she was in her last period class. Fortunately, her best friend, Raven, was in the same class and had contacted her mom to tell her what was happening. Tina's mom picked them both up from school and headed to the same hospital where she had her first child and where her mom worked. Labor didn't take so long this time. She didn't need any assistance. She felt as though her vagina was going to split in half because of the pain. Her son (Donovan Robinson) made his debut in this world after she labored for ten hours to get him here (naturally). He was very healthy and weighed six pounds, six ounces. He was twenty-one inches long, screaming at the top of his lungs. Tina knew the ropes already, being that this was her second child. She was ready to get home and care for both of her babies.

She was released from the hospital into the care of her mom. Once she got home, she started her daily routine. This consisted of breast/bottle feeding, changing diapers, washing clothes, burping, rocking crying babies to sleep, homework, and more sleepless nights. Taking care of two babies was no easy task, and there were many times that Tina would cry with exhaustion along with her babies. There were times when she wanted to just quit, but she had these two beautiful babies relying on her. Tina's mom was serious and adamant about her physically taking care of her own kids and was not going to let her take the coward's way out. She was beginning to believe that no one would want her since she already had two kids, and if they did, it would only be for sex. In the back of her mind, she felt this way. She thought that guys would see her as already damaged goods. Even though she loved herself, low self-esteem was slowly trying to take over.

She continued her education at home while being out on maternity leave. The high school provided a homebound teacher to come out to Tina's parents' house twice a week. One day to drop off schoolwork and another to pick it up. Eventually, when she made it to that six-week mark again, she was put on a stronger birth control pill. She was ready to head back to public school full time while her mom kept the kids during the day. She had overcome so many obstacles and still had several to face, but she kept on praying.

At the age of eighteen, Tina was ready to move out on her own. After months of being on the waiting list, her name finally came up for public housing. Public housing was low-income housing based on an individual's monthly income. She would be moving into a two-bedroom, one-bathroom apartment in the projects. She was extremely happy and a little nervous at the same time. She was happy because it would be her own apartment and nervous because her mom would no longer be readily available to help her with her daughter.

Tina was working part-time at a local grocery store as a cashier and wasn't making much money. She was also still attending high school. Her mom had no problem with keeping her daughter if she was doing something productive. But her mom would rarely watch her daughter when she wanted to just hang out with her friends and have fun. Tina was grateful that her mom sacrificed the time that she should have been sleeping, after her night time job, to care for her daughter while she continued her education.

Tina finally moved into her apartment with pieces of furniture given to her from neighbors and relatives. She and her daughter slept on twin mattresses on the floor with blankets. Tina didn't mind at all. She kept her apartment very clean as well as herself and her daughter. She had heard rumors that once she got her own place, it was going to be a whorehouse or a party house. She was stereotyped because she was young and had kids. She proved the naysayers wrong because her residence was neither of those.

Before work one afternoon, Tina stopped by a Firehouse Sub near her job and ordered herself a steak and cheese sub. The young man, Steve Reote, who fixed her sub, was very handsome. He was very tall and stout. He had a light complexion and hazel eyes. They both felt an immediate attraction. Once she paid for her sub, she sat down at the nearest booth to eat it. On his break, he joined her in her booth. They made plans to meet in a park at 2:00 PM on the upcoming Saturday to get to know each other. His break was over, so he said goodbye and went back to work. She was now done eating, so she went off to work as well.

Steve and Tina met in the park as planned. They both were dressed very well, and the attraction remained. He learned that she had two children. She learned that he was a mama's boy and still lived at home, even though he was eighteen years old. They continued talking and learning about each other's lives and families. They talked for hours. On that same day, he asked her to be his lady, and she happily accepted. They were now officially in a relationship.

Over time, Tina introduced Steve to her family. Her brothers liked him, her mother was okay with him, her stepdad was somewhat cordial, but her daughter really liked him, and that was what mattered the most. When he introduced her to his family, everyone liked her except his mom. She wanted her son to get back with his ex-girlfriend, who had previously cheated on him. This was why they were no longer together. Tina and Steve ignored their surroundings and indulged all their feelings for each other.

One night they both went to a Joe concert, he with his friends and she with hers. After the concert, they met up at Tina's apartment. It was late, and they sat up talking about the highlights of the concert while listening to the radio. He decided to stay overnight. They began to kiss and caress each other. They took their clothes off and got in the bed naked. They were supposed to just hold each other until they fell asleep, just cuddle. Then suddenly, Joe's song "I Want to Know" came on the radio and they began to make love. Tina was on a stronger birth control pill but had missed taking one pill two days prior. Steve was wearing a condom, but during their intense lovemaking, it broke. They kept going and didn't realize it had broken until he went to throw the condom in the garbage. They got dressed and were sort of panicking. She didn't want more kids anytime soon, and he wasn't ready to be a father. As they both feared, Tina was soon expecting baby number three. She had gone to a local health clinic two weeks later to have a pregnancy test done, which confirmed that she was pregnant. Raven was with her and comforted her while she cried. It was at that very moment, Tina established that her best friend would be the godmother of all her kids (present and future). Raven was elated at her role.

It was now time for Tina and Steve to tell their parents. Her parents couldn't believe she allowed herself to get pregnant again. But she was an adult living on her own now, and there wasn't much that they could do or say to her. Her mom let it be known that she would not be with her in the delivery room this time. She said, "enough is enough." His parents, especially his mom, were not happy at all and continued to insist that he get back with his ex-girlfriend, who they were enamored of. Steve had every intention of being with Tina throughout her pregnancy but eventually gave in to his mom's demands. Tina was already used to having and raising babies alone, so this was nothing new. She had gotten herself into this predicament, and she was going to take on her responsibilities. Steve went on to marry his ex, and they were looking forward to starting their own family. It's a good thing he did go his own way because the scent of his body made her sick to her stomach. He didn't stink or anything like that. Tina's nose was just on high alert, and she couldn't stand his natural body odor.

This pregnancy, like the first two, involved nausea, sore nipples, fatigue, etc. She craved pickles and vanilla ice cream this time around. She enjoyed hearing the baby's heartbeat and getting the ultrasound pictures after her appointments. She did not want to be pregnant at the time of her nineteenth birthday, but it was far too late to worry about that now. Also, she never wanted to know the sex of her baby because she wanted it to be a surprise at delivery.

Tina hated taking prenatal vitamins and the exams that entailed the doctor checking her uterus to see if she had dilated.

Tina and Raven were chilling at Tina's apartment while letting their kids play. Tina started feeling sharp pains that reminded her of contractions. She knew she was in labor but insisted that she had to clean her entire apartment and take a shower before going to the hospital. Once she was done, Raven drove her to drop off her daughter at her mom's house as well as her own daughter. Tina's mom was very serious about not being there this time when she had the baby. That was no problem because Raven was there to hold her hand and calm her down. There were times when Tina was in pain, and she would look over at Raven, and she would be sleeping or reading a book. Tina would yell her name to make her pay attention as if she was the nurse who would deliver her baby. After being there for eight hours, Tina yelled out a gut-wrenching scream while stretching out her legs and arms. She was pushing and didn't really know it. Raven alerted the doctor and nurses that she could see Tina's baby head crowning. They rushed in just in the nick of time to break her water. Two pushes later, Martin Robinson made his grand entrance. He weighed six pounds and five ounces. His length was nineteen inches. He took to breastfeeding right away. Like her other deliveries, this delivery was all natural with no pain medication or epidural. Tina decided she was done having kids and would soon get a tubal ligation.

She still wanted to finish her education and was focused on completing her schoolwork so that she could graduate on time, with her best friend. Graduation was only four months away, and she wanted to make sure that she met the necessary requirements. So she requested that the same homebound instructor that previously helped her come out again. She needed that extra help while she was out of school caring for her newborn baby for the next six weeks. When graduation day arrived, Tina was so happy to walk across the stage with her best friend. The two single mothers received their high school diplomas with much pride. Through a lot of hard work, support from family and friends, and constant prayer, they made it!

Tina, through her older brother, Darrius, met Jerome Wright two days after he got out of prison. She knew of him way back when they were younger, but she mainly played with his sister at the YMCA camp during the summer. She thought that he was very handsome. He was high yellow, had curly hair and dark blue eyes. He was eye candy, and by the way he carried himself, it was clear that he knew it. They decided to get to know each other by sleeping together, and a week later, he moved in. Tina's best friend and older brother thought it was much too soon for Jerome to be moving into her place, but she didn't care what they thought. Since Tina was in public housing, she was not supposed to have anyone living with her, other than her kids. Him living there could have gotten her evicted on the spot. It was a good thing the housing authority always announced when they were coming over for their yearly inspection, which allowed her enough time to put the chest where his clothes and shoes were stored in the trunk of her car.

Tina had fallen in love with Jerome, and he claimed to have fallen in love with her as well. He had the longest and largest penis that she had ever come across. Her lotus flower would always adjust to him, fitting him like a glove. Each time they were together making sweet music, it felt like the first time. Apparently, other women had been so satisfied with his lovemaking that he had never had to give oral sex before, but it was a must in Tina's world. Because he loved her, he wanted to try it but didn't know how. After they both took a nice hot shower together, she talked him through it. Over time he began to like it, but he never really met up to her standards. She never told him and dealt with it because he made up for it in other areas. So much so that she began playing wifey to him without a ring. She would soon find out it was without a commitment on his part either.

Part of the reason Tina loved him was that he was the adventurous and spontaneous type. Once they took a long drive to cross one of the tallest bridges (Burro Creek 2005 Bridge) in Arizona and while he was driving, he demanded that she slob on his knob. She was happy to oblige him. They were so obtuse that they didn't realize that one wrong move could have ended their lives had he caused an accident or driven off the side of the bridge. They laughed about it later and knew that had they died that day, in that way, they would have landed themselves straight in hell.

One night, Tina tied both of his hands apart, one to each post on her headboard, so that he could not touch her. They were both completely naked. She massaged his vein with her mouth until he was about to overflow and then she stopped. About five minutes later, she jumped aboard his ship and sailed until he was about to walk the plank, then she halted again. After teasing him so, she untied both of his hands, and he acted as if she had released a hungry lion from its cage. He went into her like a wild beast ready to devour her, attempting to break her back as they drifted like a high tide onto the shore.

She was about six months away from getting her tubes tied when she noticed she had missed her period. She knew from past experiences that when she missed her period, she was with child. As before, she got her best friend Raven involved. Raven went out to the nearest drugstore to buy a pregnancy test. Once she arrived back at Tina's apartment, Tina was crying and repeating, "I cannot be pregnant again." She was twenty-two years old now. She took the pregnancy test and waited for the results. She couldn't stand to look, so she had Raven look at the results. From the look on her face, she knew. Raven burst out laughing at Tina. Only she didn't find it funny at all. The test revealed that she had another bun in the oven.

After she dried her tears, she managed to get up enough nerve to tell her boyfriend, Jerome. She told him later that night in the privacy of her bedroom. He appeared happy about it. Tina was having second thoughts about keeping the baby. She doubted the sincerity of Jerome's happiness about her carrying his child. Her intuition told her that something wasn't quite right with him. Her gut feeling was correct.

Late one night when he thought she was sleeping, she caught him on the phone in the family room, talking to another woman. She had eased up the phone receiver in her bedroom where she was lying down in the bed, pretending to be asleep. He didn't even notice that she was on the line while he was whispering sweet nothings in this other woman's ear. Tina became very angry. All she could see was red. From the phone conversation, she knew that he and the other woman had been doing more than just talking. She knew he was cheating on her. All she could think was this good-for-nothing piece of crap was using the phone that she was paying for to talk to another woman. He had some nerve! She told that woman on the phone that she could have him and to come and get him.

She was thinking of a quick way to hurt him without getting physical with him. She came up with a master plan. She put him out of her apartment the next day, but before she did, she bleached most of his clothes and shoes. The very chest that he brought to her apartment when he first moved in still held all his belongings. She lifted the top layer of clothes and shoes and poured Clorox

40

bleach over everything below that level. She knew that when he opened the chest, everything would appear to be fine. She kindly dragged that chest out on her front lawn and left it there for him to pick up. She stayed locked inside the apartment when he returned because she knew he would be very angry and possibly violent when he found out what she had done. She was terrified as she peeked out of her bedroom window. She saw him walk up to his chest in her front yard, and she could see that he was sniffing around because of the fumes from the bleach. He became enraged when he figured out what she had done to him. Everything that he owned was in that chest. He began trying to break into her apartment to get at her, but he couldn't get in. Then he began kicking on her door and yelling at her, calling her ungodly names. She still would not let him in. One of her neighbors saw him causing a commotion and yelled out that they would call the police if he continued his behavior. Jerome took his chest and left.

A few weeks later Tina heard through the grapevine that Jerome had gotten two other women knocked up, including the woman that she caught him on the phone with. She couldn't believe that he had all three of them pregnant at the same time. She did not want to be a part of that circus. She also heard that he was doing illegal drugs. She worried that her baby could be born with birth defects. She didn't want to be tied to Jerome for the rest of her life. She started complaining, crying, and whining about how she was feeling and how she wasn't ready for another baby when she already had three kids. One of her nurse friends heard her one day and told her that she would help her, but she couldn't breathe a word to anyone. The next day her nurse friend gave her a pill that she brought home from work and told her to take it. Tina took the pill without asking any questions. She had no idea what that pill was, but she was desperate. A couple of days went by, and nothing happened. She went on with her life and began to prepare her mind for this new baby. She had to face the fact that this would be her fourth kid from a fourth baby father, and she would raise the child alone.

By the end of that week, Tina began to cramp and showed signs of bleeding. The next day the cramping got worse and the bleeding became heavier. She was hurting so bad that it felt like she was having a baby – but ten times worse. Her mom insisted that she go to the hospital because it sounded as if she was having a miscarriage. Her mom had experienced a miscarriage, so she knew exactly what was happening. Raven drove Tina to the hospital where she had birthed her previous kids. She was in the ER for at least two hours before she was seen. She thought for sure she was going to die that whole time, and Raven was right there being her ride-or-die friend. She was certain that God was punishing her for having taken that pill a week ago. She kept telling herself it couldn't have been that pill because something would have happened right away. It couldn't possibly work a whole week later. She even told herself that this happened because her baby father was on drugs, and his sperm was corrupted.

The guilt of it all weighed heavily on her. She prayed constantly, repenting what she had done. After being triaged, placed in a room, and being seen by a doctor, she learned that most of the baby had passed through her vaginal canal already. She was told by the doctor that she had a miscarriage. He also made a point of informing her, "You should be happy that you had a miscarriage, being that you're a single black female with three kids already." Tina was appalled and could not believe what the doctor had said to her. The doctor performed a D&C, and once she recovered, she was released from the hospital.

On the way home, she saw Jerome hanging on the corner, where most of his friends hung out to do their pharmaceutical jobs. She had Raven call him over to the car so that she could tell him what happened. First Tina lied and just told him she had a miscarriage. Then she told him the truth, that she took a pill and she believed it helped her body miscarry their baby. She wasn't surprised that he seemed to be very relieved. She was sure that he was thinking that this was one fewer baby he would have to pay child support for. He didn't have a legal job. Tina chose not to deal with him again until later in life.

She eventually got her tubes tied. She figured whoever she would meet in the future would have to already have kids. She wasn't down with being stuck with another baby from another guy. She continued to work and take care of herself as well as her kids the best way that she knew.

At the age of twenty-four, Tina met Puma Levy at a local cafe. He wasn't really her type at first, but she was nice in response to his kind gestures. He was shorter than she, standing at five feet four inches, and looked like a bodybuilder, which was not up her alley at all. He was such a charmer, though, and was laying it on thick to win her over. After running into him every other day at the cafe, she became intrigued by him, mainly because he was an older man. He was ten years older to be exact. He was very consistent in pursuing her, showering her with a lot of attention, which she loved. She felt that meeting a handsome, nicely groomed, always- smelling-good man like this was too good to be true. So she asked him, "Are you married?"

He responded, "No, I am not married; I am divorced." Tina asked for proof, such as divorce papers. He quickly said that his divorce papers were packed away and that he would show them to her later. She should have gone with her gut feeling that he was not being truthful.

One evening, about two months later, when they both were walking out of the cafe, Puma held the door for Tina to walk through, reaching in to plant his lips right on hers. His kiss was so sensual that he stole her heart at that very moment. He then invited her over to his house for a romantic candlelight dinner, with a little peach Moscato. He was wearing a nice navy-blue suit, and she was wearing a short, coral, tight-fitting dress that fell slightly off her shoulders. They both were looking fly. That night she found out that he was a neat freak and kept his house very tidy. There was no evidence of a wife or kids based on the pictures throughout his house. So she felt that she could let down her guard and open up to him. She then found out that Puma wasn't rich, but he was well off. He was a stockbroker who worked at a renowned brokerage firm. That night after dinner, they took their friendship to the next level, inside his bedroom. He made love to her without using much of his hands at all. He only used his tongue. Tina could tell that his goal was to blow her mind with this tactic, in which he succeeded. This was not her first time receiving oral sex. However, this by far was the best she'd ever had. He had taken her places intimately that she had never gone before and showed her things that she had never experienced before. Not to mention giving her multiple orgasms back to back. He said that her scent was amazing! He was an exotic lover and never had to worry about her even thinking about cheating on him. It was never going to happen. They didn't go all the way that night, which made her want him even more. She was smitten with the man. He was husband material. The next morning, he hit Tina with those three magic words (I love you). She felt the same way but wouldn't dare be the first to say it. From that day forward, they were a happy couple and were with each other every day.

He met her family, including her kids, and they all loved him. Puma loved Tina so much that he decided to get her first name tattooed across his upper back, between his shoulder blades. Tina could not believe that he had done such a thing. Because she loved him too, a week later she got a tattoo of his first name right in the arch of her lower back to prove her love and loyalty to him. They were so in love. They were inseparable. She was his, and he was hers. Only later she would find out that he belonged to someone else.

A month later, he proposed to her in the café where they first met in front of two of their friends, Todd Gaye and Raven. Tina had no clue that this was about to happen. They sat at their usual table. She thought that they were just having a little brunch with their besties, who just happened to be in on the surprise. Then, suddenly, his best friend Todd stood up and began to sing their favorite song, "Breathe Again" by Toni Braxton. He asked her to dance with him, which she did. She looked over and saw Raven crying and was wondering what was going on. Puma then dropped down to one knee, took out a ring box from his pocket, opened it, and asked her, "Will you marry me?" Tina screamed and accepted his proposal with no hesitation. She was so happy!

They began to talk about possibly having a baby. Puma knew that Tina's tubes were tied. He was excited and was willing to foot the bill to have her tubes untied, which could be very risky. Tina did the research and found a local doctor who was willing to do the procedure for eleven thousand dollars. Family and friends tried to talk Tina out of getting the surgery done and thought she was crazy for wanting to have another baby. This would be his first child (at least that's what he told her), and he desperately wanted a baby boy to carry on his last name. Tina ignored all the negativity that her family and friends threw her way. She set up an appointment with the doctor to go ahead and have the surgery done. She had no doubt that he would one day marry her and didn't feel the need to pressure him to do so.

Prior to the surgery date, Puma had to have his sperm count checked to make sure the odds for Tina having a baby after the procedure were very high. At his first attempt, in the hospital's specified restroom for this to take place, Tina was there to help him out with a little hand action. In the heat of the moment, Puma quickly bent her over the sink, lifted her dress up and slid her panties down, just enough so that they would drop to the floor. He then proceeded to take her until he was about to ejaculate, then grabbed the specimen cup to release himself in. He turned it in to one of the nurses on duty that day. Unfortunately, the test results came back contaminated. Both of their bodily fluids were in the specimen cup, and the doctors knew what had transpired. On Puma's second attempt, he had to go it alone, with the help of a magazine. He was properly able to give the nurse an uncontaminated sample of his sperm. His test results came back perfect, with a healthy sperm count.

After her surgery, which was like a cesarean, she had to wait six weeks before they could try to have a baby. When she went back for her follow up after six weeks, she learned that they had run dye through her tubes during surgery to make sure her tubes were functional. She also found out that the doctor who had done her tubal ligation surgery was looking out for her and her future. Instead of permanently tying her tubes (via cutting, burning, clipping, etc.), there were plastic circular clamps placed around them. This gave Tina a better chance at conceiving. All her current doctor had to do was remove the plastic clamps from around her tubes and clean up the scar tissue. She then was ready to go. She was told that she would have a fifty/fifty chance of getting pregnant now. Tina and Puma tried to conceive several times after her six weeks checkup, with no luck.

One day she came home from work to him sniffing a pair of her panties that he had gotten out of her dirty clothes basket. At first, she thought it was a little bizarre, but once she saw that he was turned on and was patiently waiting to pounce on her, she became aroused as well. After giving her a full body massage, Puma made love to her like he never had before. To Tina, it was pure ecstasy from the immaculate foreplay all the way down to the creamy white showers. This man had the whole package from head to toe. It was like they both put their souls into it, and they were intertwined. Afterward, he told her that he had just given her his baby boy. Tina just kind of laughed it off, and they cuddled until they fell asleep.

As time went on, she began to experience feelings that she remembered from her previous pregnancies, including missing her period. She was ecstatic. They both went to see Tina's obstetrician to have a urine and blood pregnancy test done. Both tests came back positive. Tina and Puma were so overjoyed! Tina just knew that this fairytale was real, and they would live happily ever after. Puma was a great soon-to-be father. He was with her through her entire pregnancy, rubbing her feet, her back, and her stomach. He even talked to the baby by talking to her stomach.

The pregnancy was quite easy compared to the others. They continued having mesmerizing encounters up until the day she went into labor. In fact, she went into labor as a result of the legion of pinnacles she reached that day. Tina realized that she was in labor and felt the need to clean her apartment and take a shower. Although she and Puma were together all the time, they kept separate residences. They would alternate staying at one another's cribs. Once she was done showering, she begged him to take her to the hospital because she was in so much discomfort.

He drove her to the same hospital where her other kids were born and where her mom worked in the morgue. Tina had had all her kids naturally thus far, without any pain medicine. She wanted to do the same with this baby. After the nurse broke her water, her labor became intense. She couldn't take the pain anymore and screamed for an epidural, which she was given. Tina felt no more pain, only pressure. Had she'd known it would be this easy, she would have requested an epidural when she was in labor with her other children. It was so laid back that she really didn't even know when to push. The nurse had to tell her when. After about seven pushes and pure fatigue, Demetrius Levy was born. He weighed six pounds, six ounces and was twenty-two inches long. Puma was so proud of his son. He was the first person to hold him. Demetrius had his first poop while his father was holding him in his arms, which brought him to much laughter. He was the only child of Tina's to carry his father's last name. They had discussed that if the surgical procedure worked and they were successful at having a baby, she would get fixed again, permanently. So, Tina had her tubes tied again, right after delivering the baby. They did it through her vagina/uterus, while she was still numb from the waist down, from the epidural. Three days later, she and her baby boy were released from the hospital. Puma was there to drive them home to Tina's apartment, to meet the rest of her kids and bond. He was a good father and good man.

Six months later they had set a date for getting married and were planning their wedding. She was ready. He believed in God, and they shared the same faith. She and he shared the same religious views but weren't quite walking the walk/living that lifestyle. She remembered that he had never produced his divorce papers for her, so she demanded to see them now. He came up with the same excuse. She began to wonder, what was he hiding? She was fed up and decided to ask his best friend Todd, "Why is Puma being so shady and mysterious?"

Todd called her a fool for getting involved with a man who hadn't upfront shown his divorce decree. He said, "That was a sign that he was still married right in your face." She was heartbroken and boldly confronted Puma that very same day. All he could say was, "I love you, and I'm sorry!" He was still married, and on top of that, he had three little girls, each two years apart, with his wife. They had been separated for a while because she didn't like living in Phoenix. She had moved back to her home in Seattle, Washington.

He said he had wanted to tell Tina, but he wanted her so bad and didn't want to mess up his chances of getting her. He never intended on marrying her. He was just stringing her along for the ride and to have his son. They held each other and just cried because they knew it was over. Tina believed that he was only crying because he'd gotten caught. She was crying because she was hurt and wanted to kill him but couldn't. He'd played her for a fool. He had hurt her to the core.

Puma ended up moving to Seattle with his wife and kids to make their marriage work, leaving her alone to raise his child. As time went on, he attempted to be in Demetrius' life as much as possible, calling him every now and then.

Tina went on with her life. She continued to work, this time in an office job, making a little more money than before. Her focus was on taking care of her kids and home. She still could receive public assistance to curb some of her expenses and relied on her mom for her babysitting needs. She was mad at herself because she saw all the red flags in the beginning but chose to ignore them. Secretly, she still yearned for his kiss, touch, and love. He would have been perfect for her if only he wasn't a pathological liar. In her eyes and in her heart, he was the one that got/walked away. Eventually, she prayed her way through the heartbreak and continued to hold her head high, despite what rumors she heard or what foul names she was called. Puma kept in contact with Tina's parents and other kids via phone calls, which was always very awkward for everyone involved.

Tina's eagerness to do better for herself and her kids forced her to think of their future. She had to make some changes. Those positive changes made her think about achievements. She set goals even when she didn't want to. Some of those goals she wasn't sure she could accomplish but was willing to try. Some of those goals just happened upon her. Once she started something, she didn't like to stop until she finished it. That often led to a successful ending, monetarily and gave her higher self-esteem.

"For the Son of Man came to seek and to save the lost"
(New International Version, Luke. 19.10).

My Heart

I carried my heart full of love in my hand and handed it straight to you. You took my heart and bruised it so, giving it back to me black and blue.

I've walked around seventy-six months now wondering why I haven't truly moved on. Although over time I've accomplished a lot, my heart still sings that same song.

A glimmer of hope it thought it'd find, but little did it know, today was the day that my heart decided to finally let you go!

Chapter 3 - Achievements

≈

Tina had few goals in life because she really didn't see herself getting past public housing and the welfare system. She had so many kids at a young age and had a grim outlook on life. Even though she had a desire to learn, she didn't see a way out of her situation. Little did she know, education would be her way out. Even during life's storms, she began to use education as an escape from her reality. She knew there was much more to life than public assistance (housing, WIC, food stamps, and cash assistance). She looked around at her surroundings and knew that this was not her destiny. Although she was grateful for what she had, she could not stay in her current predicament forever.

Tina's greatest achievements were her children. She didn't understand this when they were babies, but as she got older, she began to understand it a little. She had been so fixated on not wanting kids at such a young age since she was just a child herself. She had thought her life was over when she delivered her first child. She just couldn't comprehend why God would grant her such perfect gifts at those times in her life. Couldn't he see that she was too young and had no clue about what she was doing? She was a baby raising babies. Tina's human mind could not grasp the concept that God chose her as His vessel to bring these beautiful individuals into this world, all of which he had created. She started to embrace the fact that even though she didn't understand the whys of it all, she knew that God made no mistakes and was in control! Tina's kids taught her about responsibility. They taught her how to love. They showed her what true and unconditional love really meant. She didn't think that she could ever love someone that much. Also, she knew that she had to set a good example for her kids because they were watching her every move and soaking up what they saw, like sponges. Tina's kids would probably say that she was a strict mom and believed in disciplining them. She felt that she had to because she was determined not to allow her kids to fall into what statistics had planned for kids who grew up in a single mother's household. Even though God chose her to be her children's mother, He knew that she could not take care of them all on her own. So, He surrounded her with a support system. Those supporters came in the form of her mom, her best friend, her relatives, public assistance, etc. That old saying that "it takes a village to raise a child" was so true. Over time, her kids' individual personalities begin to flourish. This helped Tina to embark on the real world. They were her reason for living, providing (with what she had) and ensuring that their futures became brighter.

Another one of her achievements was graduating from Phoenix Lovelace High School and receiving her diploma. It may not have been a big deal to some, but it was a triumph to her. She marched across that stage with her chest stuck out, shoulders back, and her head held high. She was very proud. She was proud because one day she would be able to tell her kids that she graduated at the age of nineteen, with three kids. Her GPA wasn't the greatest, but she reached her goal. Her mom was very proud of her too because she had dropped out of high school when she was in the eleventh grade. She was a young mother as well. Tina was a little disappointed that her stepfather didn't attend her graduation, but she quickly got over it, based on how he treated her in the past.

Tina and Raven decided to put together a very last-minute cookout to celebrate their great accomplishment. Raven marched across the stage too that day. The cookout was scheduled for five o'clock that evening. They invited a few of their friends and associates and asked that they all bring a dish. They all hung out, talked about good times, laughed, cried, and talked about their futures. Most of Tina's friends/associates revealed that they were heading off to college come fall. As stated earlier, Tina had a burning desire to learn, but she hated school. She had no intentions of ever going to college.

Her next achievement was when she found herself enrolling in a law-enforcement-related program at Phoenix Love Technical Institute (PLTI). She signed up for a nine-month forensic science program because she wanted to take after her stepfather, who was in law enforcement. As stated in Chapter One, her stepfather was a sheriff at the local sheriff's department. She still worked at her office job and worked hard toward receiving her forensic science certification. Her work ethic, which developed over time (from being a single mom and observing her parents' work ethic), contributed to her being a hard worker and focused. Tina scored well on her homework assignments and tests. She completed the program early at the eight-month mark. She requested that PLTI send her certificate in the mail. She thought that this would be the end of the road for her as far as education.

She discovered that she needed more than a certificate to get a law enforcement job. She needed to enlist into the Phoenix Love Police Academy (PLPA), which was about five hours away from her hometown. Tina took the necessary entrance exam, drug test, background check, endurance test, and physical to get into the program. She passed everything with flying colors. She took an oath of training so that she could serve and protect her fellow cadets as well as the community. The PLPA program was an intense thirteen-week training program. This program consisted of a lot of classes, obstacle courses, teamwork/bonding, weapons, marching, cadences, and physical training (PT). She was excited and nervous about starting. She left her kids home in her mother's care under temporary custody during the training. She knew that she had to complete this program because she was determined to make a better life for herself and her kids. Also, she had given up her office job for this opportunity.

Tina met a lot of people from different walks of life. She built some awesome bonds, ones that she would still have after the academy. Although she had a difficult time getting through the program, she enjoyed her time there. Her team started out with sixty cadets but ended with forty-five on graduation day. Fifteen cadets could not pass the final PT test and had to retake it. Graduation day came around, and Tina had no family to attend, due to finances. She was a little let down. However, she still graduated with pride. She was sure that her stepfather would be proud of her now, once he saw her certificate of completion. In her mind, they were kind of on the same level and on the same team. She was so ready to get back home to see her children and family.

Once she got home, everyone seemed proud of her accomplishment, except her stepfather. He was still being his usual self, standoffish, and barely talked to her. She later found out from a family friend that her stepfather was very proud of her and bragged about her being a policewoman, which made her heart smile.

Shortly after graduating, Tina began to work for a local police department, which was literally across the street from the sheriff department where her stepdad worked. She was very happy and ready to get onto the streets of her community. She was ready to fight crime. She had no idea that her fighting crime would be writing tickets for parking violations only.

She would much later be promoted to policing the streets but was instructed to only participate in family-related crimes that involved kids. Tina thought that this was perfect for her until the day she was shot in the leg by a ten-year-old boy. She was called out to a house where a mother reported that her son was being violent with her. She was informed that the kid had some behavior problems. She was trained for this and knew that she could handle the kid in question.

When Tina arrived, she saw the kid threatening to kill his mom with a butcher knife that he had gotten from the kitchen. She found out that the mom wouldn't let the kid go to a party with his older friends because he was too young. He didn't agree with what his mom said, and he just flipped out. Tina tried talking the kid down because it was obvious that the mom had no control of her son whatsoever. With success, Tina took the knife from the kid. Everything appeared to be in order. As she turned to leave, the kid grabbed a gun out of the waist of his pants, aimed, and shot her in the left leg. Later she found out that he was aiming for her foot. She had to call for backup. The kid was arrested and taken to a juvenile detention center. Tina was taken in an ambulance to the nearest hospital. The bullet went straight through her leg, hitting no major arteries, which made her recovery minimal.

Tina had an epiphany. She did not want to be a beat police officer anymore. She now wanted to be a homicide detective. That meant she had to go back to school, which she tried so very hard to avoid.

Tina prayed a lot during this time. In fact, she credited her making it through the Academy and not bleeding out when she was shot in the leg to God. Even though she had faith, she wasn't happy with God's allowance of bad things to happen in her life. She just didn't quite understand but had no choice but to live. The bottom line was, His will would be done, regardless.

Tina's best friend (Raven) talked her into enrolling into college because she was enrolling too, and they could take classes together. They were both working toward obtaining their associates of arts degrees in general studies. One of the classes they took together was Introduction to Speech. They were assigned to write a speech based on a poem that they liked and could relate to their lives. Tina chose the poem, "Still I Rise" by Maya Angelou, which brought her to tears in front of the entire class as she read it. The excerpt that she took from the poem was, "You may shoot me with your words, / You may cut me with your eyes, / You may kill me with your hatefulness, / But still, like air, I'll rise" (Angelou, 1978). Later during the semester, Raven decided that college was not for her and dropped out. Tina wanted to drop out too but was told that if she did, she would have to pay back to the college all the money from the Pell grant that she'd received. Tina didn't have the funds to do that, so she stayed enrolled and continued through college until she eventually graduated. This was one of the best days of her life. Her kids, Raven, and her mom attended her graduation. She was so shocked that she made it that she decided to continue to get her bachelor's degree, which was one of the best decisions she could have made.

Tina applied for and was accepted into the Phoenix Love Community College Criminal Justice Bachelor's program. This would be an auspicious start to her career as a homicide detective. She enrolled in two classes per semester because that was all that she could handle while still working full time as a policewoman. She met some amazing people on her journey to getting her bachelor's, some of whom she would remain friends with even after graduation. Also, she networked with some bigwigs at work, who could help catapult her career once she had her degree in hand. One good thing about Tina's job was they would reimburse her monetarily for taking classes as long as she received a grade of a C or better. So she could get back and pocket the Pell grant money that she'd previously received. After countless hours of homework, discussions, team projects, and writing essays, she finally made it to graduation day. Again, her family was there, but this time was different. Her stepdad was there, and she was so happy and proud. Because Tina now had her bachelor's degree in criminal justice, she received a nice raise at work. She was making a substantial amount of money now, and she moved into a better apartment and got off of all public assistance. That alone gave her a humbling sense of pride. She later shadowed a homicide detective who was in her precinct to see if this was what she really wanted to do. She did this for about two months, for at least one complete day a week. She enjoyed it and wanted to continue her education to secure a foot in the door with this career.

Tina enrolled in the Phoenix Love University Criminal Justice Master's program online. She was really excited about this program because it was only sixteen months long and was thirty-six credits total. At the graduate level, she had to apply for student loans, which she received. She ordered her books online and had them mailed directly to her apartment, just in time for classes to start. She still very much disliked school, especially the reading and writing part of it. In this program, she had to write an essay a week, anywhere from one to ten pages. This was a big challenge for her, as was test-taking, but she succeeded. She had no choice but to succeed because she knew that if she got more than one C, she could be put out of the program.

Tina maintained As and Bs throughout the semesters. Through all the stress, she received a lot of encouragement from her family, friends, and co-workers. She practically quit college every week – every time she looked at the syllabus for that week's assignment. She was jovial that she had neared the end of her program and would soon graduate. Her graduation was a big deal because she knew this was it as far as her academic excursion. She wanted everyone to attend and witness her walk across that stage. Unfortunately, her mom and stepdad could not attend her graduation this time because they both had the flu and were stuck in the house. It was okay, though, because her kids and Raven were there to cheer her on. Tina graduated with a high GPA. She had no clue that all that reading and writing that she'd had to do to acquire her master's degree would prepare her for the next two chapters in her life. Her master's degree landed her a promotion as a lead homicide detective at her current precinct, and she would later go on to create a short film as her side hustle.

One of Tina's recent achievements was the writing and directing of a short, low-budget film called *The African Queen Reigns*. This film basically depicted how women of color were influential to their kings, family, friends, and community, without stereotyping them. It also reflected on why black people (Tina's people) suffered so on this earth and why they had been oppressed for so long. She believed that it was because they were the chosen ones, the true Hebrew Israelites. She felt very savant at times because of her belief. Tina spent three months writing the film. Then she spent another three months auditioning family, friends, co-workers, etc., to make it all come to life. She wanted to see her ideas on paper come to fruition. She needed a cast, production, audio, lighting, stunt doubles, automation, costumes, music, etc. She needed all of this but at a reasonable price and, in some cases, free. It took her so long to complete because she was trying to do all of this while still working a full-time job. She was juggling everything but was determined to make it all work.

Once the film was completed, it was shown at local boys and girls clubs in the community. Tina was hoping that someone important would see it and want to invest in helping her get the short film to the big screen. She wanted her film to juxtapose costumes of traditional African and modern-day culture. Her hard work eventually paid off, and her film was shown at the next Sundance Festival, in front of many celebrities. She was so gratified by her little film. She considered it to be the little film that could, so to speak. This made her confidence about what she could do shoot through the roof. She could picture herself one day living an opulent lifestyle. She began to reminisce on how she didn't always have a high level of self-love/worth.

"I can do all things through Christ who strengthens me" (New King James Version, Phil. 4.13).

Chapter 4 - Self-Love/Worth

≈

Tina had always loved herself but not as she should have or how she deserved. She really couldn't have loved herself if she gave herself so freely to different men, who really didn't care about her at all. Over time, she slept with so many men that she couldn't even keep count, including her babies' fathers. They just happened to be the ones that got her knocked up.

Tina raised her kids on her own (with the help of her support system, of course) and pretty much kept to herself, so she was somewhat of a loner. She didn't have to have or want people around her all the time. She wasn't a nymphomaniac, so she didn't need sex all the time. In fact, there were times when she would go months without it. She was just a product of her environment as far as what she was exposed to at such a young age. Some saw this as an indication that she had low self-esteem, but Tina viewed it as she was just having a bad day. Well, she considered herself to have had a lot of bad days.

She made the mistake of seeing the potential in a man, instead of looking at what he was presenting to her at the moment. Because she was shown what she thought was love, many times she overlooked the red flags that were right in front of her. She was finally realizing that what a man was when she met him was usually what he would be in life, period.

Tina began talking to her ex-boyfriend Jerome Wright, the father of her fourth baby (miscarried with help). She was talking to him again because he briefly showed her that he had changed and that his change was for the better. She quickly found out that he was only talking to her because he needed/wanted a new place to stay. He was currently living with a woman whom he was using for a place to stay and financial security. Basically, someone that could take care of him. At least that was what he told Tina. He never referred to her as his girlfriend, so Tina was not sure what she was to him. He claimed that this woman was feeding his drug/alcohol habits and was easy to run over/use, which was why he needed a new place to stay. Unfortunately, Tina found out that he was trying to use her as well. That was not Tina's mode of operation.

At that moment, she came to an important crossroads in her life. That crossroads was that she was fed up with men trying to use her, fed up with their lying and cheating. She decided to take a journey of celibacy. She had tried celibacy once before and only made it to a year. This journey, as before, was a very difficult one to start. After all she loved having sex. But she knew she had to make some changes. She knew that she loved herself, but she needed to modify her life for her outcome to become a bigger, better, and brighter destiny. This time she vowed to do things God's way because her way always messed things up. Her plan was to wait until marriage to have sex this go around. Tina's celibacy journey turned into ten years and still counting.

During that time, she began to seek God by praying, fasting, and studying His holy word (the Bible). She wanted her relationship with Him to be closer and stronger than before. She had strayed from Him many times in the past. Even though she tried very hard to stay on the right track, she still found herself sometimes giving into the temptation of masturbation. She then would immediately pray and ask for forgiveness. This was just a reminder to her that she couldn't do this walk alone. She learned quickly that even the strong get weak. She thought that as each year passed being able to sustain celibacy would be that much easier. She was incorrect about that assumption. Over time, Tina could tell that her mind and vision grew a lot clearer. She could spot users from a mile away. She also invested time into her education (received her bachelors and masters as referenced in Chapter Three). She put in much effort to avoid certain things that would make her think of sex, such as movies, music, books, social media, etc. That helped her a lot, but there were times when she would allow those thoughts to creep back in, just to satisfy her flesh. On different occasions, Tina did everything that she could to do wrong (as far as planning to hook up with an ex), but it just didn't work out. She felt that it was God's way of saying, "I told you to sit your butt down somewhere and wait!"

God began to transform Tina on the inside. Not only was He healing her heart, but He was healing her mind, her body, and spirit. She was beginning to truly love herself more as well as others. She was learning what self-love/worth really meant, and she loved the woman that she was becoming. She still had a bit of an issue with trust, though. God wasn't done working on her yet. A man whom she was getting to know once told her that he wanted a woman who would trust him right off the bat. Their relationship didn't go any further because Tina believed that to gain someone's trust, a person should have to show that he or she was trustworthy.

Tina soon realized that having self-love and knowing her self-worth was like not wanting to be alone but being okay with being alone. She knew that she had God in her life. She rested in knowing that He knew and had in mind what was best for her. She strived to be a virtuous woman. She learned to be patient and wait on Him.

Tina loved knowing her self-worth. She was never really a materialistic person. She was not a fashionista, wasn't into jewelry, flowers, etc. She was not a flashy person. She considered herself to be a plain Jane. She was good if the clothes she was wearing were clean, her hair was done to her liking, she smelled good and looked presentable. However, she did make sure her kids had and were dressed in the finer things. Acknowledging her self-love/worth came from God's love for her. He planted a seed of forgiveness within her, watered it, and watched it grow.

"Therefore if anyone is in Christ, he is a new creation. The old things have passed away. Behold, all things have become new" (World English Bible, 2 Cor. 5.17).

Chapter 5 - Forgiveness

≈

Tina found herself asking God for forgiveness many times, in many different situations throughout her life. She knew that if God had forgiven her for her various sins that she had to forgive others, as a Christian. She understood that forgiving others was more for her sanity and well-being than for them. Forgiveness was the key for her to truly experience freedom. Forgiving others who had hurt her in some shape, form, or fashion was difficult for her at times. Most importantly of all, Tina had to learn to forgive herself. She was not one to hold grudges. She understood that everybody had their own battles to fight. Because she had God, she knew that He would fight her battles for her. She believed that life was too short, and no one was ever promised a tomorrow. She began to reflect on the many people that she forgave (including herself) and why, in the order that she remembered the events happening. Also, she let some of those people know (via text) that she prayed that they forgive her as well for anything that she may have said and/or done to hurt them.

Tina forgave her maternal uncle (Triston), the musician, for persuading her (at the age of eight) into playing a game of jacking him off. She didn't forgive him when the event happened. It was years later in life, once she found out that he had a drug problem. He had a crack cocaine addiction and basically took advantage of her and her naïveté. She had trusted him. This wasn't an excuse that she used to forgive him, but it was a peek into his world as to why he may have done what he did.

Tina forgave her maternal uncle (Chris) for groping her and grinding on her in her parents' house when she was only nine years old. She knew that he was affiliated with a street gang and had a history of drug abuse. He drank alcohol and used hard street drugs such as heroine, crack cocaine, powder cocaine, etc. His brain cells were so burnt that he probably couldn't remember what he had done anyway. Again, this was another way that Tina tried to comprehend why she was his target that day.

Tina chose to forgive her paternal cousin (Randell), the middle school math teacher, for cleverly trying to pull her pants down that day when she came over to borrow a cup of sugar. Perhaps he was just a pervert because much later in life, she learned that he had done this to other female neighbors back then. No one ever reported him, and it was far too late now.

Her paternal cousin (Chester) was forgiven by her for his sexual innuendos. At the age of eleven, she never gave him any indication that it was okay for him to approach her in that manner. Perhaps, it was his sixteen-year-old hormones in full bloom. Even though she forgave him, she still gave him the side eye when he would try to hug her for too long. Tina thought that maybe because he had protected her in certain situations, he felt that she owed him something.

Tina forgave herself for getting involved in a fight that was between her brother Darrius and his friend (Deon Matters). Darrius and Deon were fighting over some guy stuff, but Tina saw that Deon's sister jumped in. Tina decided to jump into the fight to help her brother as well. Deon slung Tina down to the ground hard. She saw a beer bottle on the ground, grabbed it, jumped up and hit Deon over the head with it. That move ended the fight in its entirety. Tina was scared and thought she was going to jail for what she had done. Fortunately, Deon didn't call the police on her and didn't press charges. She realized that had she hit him on his temple, the fight could have ended differently. She apologized to Deon and his sister for everything that took place, and they became friends.

Tina forgave herself for getting into a fight with a schoolmate (Veronica Sky) after school one day. They were still at the bus stop. They were the same age, but Veronica was shorter than Tina. Veronica allowed her friends to boost her up to fight Tina. She attempted to ignore Veronica for as long as she could, but it didn't work. Tina was provoked to the max. She snapped, picked Veronica up off the ground, and body-slammed her. Veronica began to have a seizure, and Tina didn't know what to do. She was afraid and just stood there. One of Veronica's friends turned her over onto her side, and another ran to get help from her family. Tina was very sorry and ran home. She found out later that Veronica had a history of having seizures and that thanks to her friend's quick thinking, she would be just fine. Tina and Veronica became friends after that and acted as if the fight never happened. She was grateful that Veronica didn't die on her that day.

Tina forgave Persia Rogue (adult) for jumping on her because she was fighting her sister (Debra Rogue). Tina and Debra were a year apart and were fighting on the school bus one day as it was pulling in to drop them off near home. Persia heard the noise and saw what was happening through the windows of the bus. She saw that Tina had gotten the best of her sister, and she was not happy with that outcome. She forced Debra to fight Tina again, when it was obvious that she didn't want to fight anymore. Tina didn't want to fight anymore either. At that point, Persia jumped in the fight and beat Tina up. Tina's mom came to the bus stop to make her come home and stop fighting. Persia started saying mean things to Tina's mom, like her husband was a cheater, and she cursed her mom out. Tina's mom snapped and beat Persia up. The only reason Tina's mom got involved was because Persia was running her mouth. Tina couldn't believe that an adult was fighting her sister's battles. The fight ended because other adults stepped in and broke it up. Persia and Debra later apologized for their choice of words and actions.

It took Tina a little longer to forgive her stepfather, but she finally did. Again, this was the only father she knew. She couldn't even muster up an excuse for him for what he had mentally and spiritually done to her. His abuse was the defining moment that cemented her disconnect from all men from that day forward. God had to intervene in this matter for her. She and her stepfather are not where they used to be, but they are in a better place and have come a mighty long way.

She also forgave him for beating her badly one day outside in public, in front of all the neighbors, with an extension cord. He beat her because she talked back to him. He took every frustration that he ever had in life out on Tina that day with that extension cord. He beat her so bad that she walked with a limp for the next three days, from a gash on the back of her left lower thigh that would not stop bleeding. She should have been taken to the hospital to get stitches, but instead was nursed by her best friend's parents. It was very odd that no one tried to help her while she was beaten. Nor did anyone call the police. Tina remembered walking passed her stepfather after she was bandaged up and noticed that he was wearing a pair of dark shades. She then noticed he had shed a tear or two. She was very angry with him because she knew that he realized that he had gone too far. Till this day, she still has that mark on the back of her left lower thigh and an extension cord welt scar on the front of her left upper thigh.

She also forgave her stepfather for not really being there for her or his real kids (her brothers). As far as she could remember, her stepfather practically lived in the bedroom. The only time he came out of the bedroom was to work, eat, use the bathroom, take a shower, and/or discipline them. Tina had always heard that having a two-parent household was essential. She begged to differ because she had a two-parent household, but her stepfather was not there. He was there physically, but that was it.

Tina forgave herself for, at one point, blaming her mom for her stepfather's actions when she was twelve years old. She felt that her mom should have been working the day shift at the hospital's morgue, instead of the graveyard shift. She felt that her mom should have been home with her husband at night like most normal married couples were. She didn't realize that her mom couldn't just change shifts when she felt like it. She didn't understand that her mom needed the extra money that she was making on that shift to help keep their household in order. Most of all, Tina didn't tell her mom what happened, and her mom couldn't read her mind.

Tina forgave her paternal cousin (Jersey) for taking advantage of her by taking her virginity. He knew better, even if she didn't. He had the audacity to ask her as an adult in passing (after she graduated from the police academy), "Would you give me some?" He was acting as if what they had done in the past was nothing and normal. She told him, "No and don't ever ask me nothing like that again." He agreed and drove off.

Tina forgave herself for falling in love with her cousin (Jersey). She also forgave herself for allowing him to explore her flower bomb. Even though he was an adult and knew better, she chose to forgive him for everything that he had done. She had to, to have peace within.

Tina forgave her aunt (Reba) for not believing her when she told her that her cousin (Jersey) was feeling her butt. She felt that had her aunt believed her that could have prevented the future events that took place between her and her cousin. She might then have had the nerve to tell her parents.

Tina forgave her aunt (Valerie Nugget) for starting and spreading the rumor that she was pregnant by her own cousin (Jersey). She was just trying to start drama with Tina's mom. She even went as far to say that Tina's daughter was named after Jersey's grandmother. There were people who believed her aunt. They only came around to see who her baby resembled.

Her aunt Valerie even accused her of flirting with her husband one day out on their front porch. It was her husband that was trying to come on to Tina. Tina said to him, "Aren't you my aunt's husband?" Once he realized that she knew who he was, he then tried to turn the tables on her. The bottom line was, her uncle flirted with anyone who walked by their house and was wearing a skirt.

Tina believed that her cousin (Jersey) possibly thought that her daughter Keyla was indeed his because of the way he looked at her daughter one day, when they all attended a relative's funeral. She shook his hand, but he didn't look her in the face. He was too busy looking at Keyla, perhaps to try and find any resemblance to him. She assured him that her daughter belonged to Leonard and for him to not even try it. That was their last conversation and last time seeing each other in person.

She couldn't believe that he went on to get married and have kids of his own. In the back of Tina's mind, she wondered if he had touched his own daughter in inappropriate ways or had even taken her virginity. If he did, it probably would have been swept under the rug. Ironically, he went on to become a preacher as well. To each his own.

Tina forgave her real father (Lifeline) for being locked up in prison and not being there for her. She heard the many horror stories about how his hot temper landed him behind bars. She was told that he got his moniker Lifeline because if he liked a person, that person would live, but if he didn't like a person, that person would have lost their last lifeline. Translation, either he or someone he sent would end that person's life. Tina found that she had blamed him a lot for not protecting her. She used to feel that if he had been in her life, she wouldn't have gone through half of the stuff that she'd gone through. She eventually started writing him letters, visiting him in prison, and accepting his phone calls to attempt to build some type of relationship with him. After all, he was her blood.

Tina forgave all her babies' fathers (Leonard, Frank, Steve, Jerome, and Puma) for leaving her alone to raise their children. She was very bitter at first. Eventually, she let it go. She wanted to be the best mom that she could be, and she couldn't do that holding on to that toxic waste. She didn't want to be miserable, sitting around hoping that one of them would be in her life for the long haul. So she made the best of her life with what she had. However, she did take three of her babies' fathers to court for child support, which added to the village.

Tina forgave her first child's father (Leonard) for not accepting his responsibility earlier in his child's life. She also forgave him for telling people that she threw herself on him. It was obvious that he was trying to save his reputation and image in the eyes of his family. He was the one who suggested the game of doctor in the first place. He could have shut the game down by suggesting playing

73

something else or he could have continued hanging out with his friends. Not to mention, he was the adult in this matter; she was only thirteen at that time. She remembered later in life, as their daughter got older and she sued him for child support, he said, "Tina was just all about the money." Tina needed help taking care of their daughter that did not include living off public assistance or the little money she made from working. Also, if she was just all about the money, she would have sued him for child support as soon as their daughter was born. Instead, she lied about his whereabouts to keep him in the clear. Out of eighteen years, he was only required to pay child support during the last three. Tina believed he got a pretty good deal.

Tina forgave herself for blaming her first child (Keyla) for what she thought was the end of her entire life. She thought that she wouldn't be able to do anything, go anywhere, or be anybody. Her daughter had messed up her beautiful fourteen-year-old body during that time. She remembered thinking that she would never be able to meet a man when she got older because not only was her stomach stretched out of shape, but she felt that her vagina was as well. She didn't understand how her delicate vagina could go back to its original state. In all actuality, Tina's daughter saved her life. She now had a purpose. Her daughter was her responsibility, and she had to care for her the best way she knew how. She had no time to worry about herself anymore. She knew that this new bundle of life was counting on her. There's no doubt in Tina's mind that had she not had her daughter, she would have succumbed to her surroundings, which were not great.

Tina forgave Rhonda and Belinda, her two best friends at the time, for turning their backs on her when she was pregnant with her first child. This was when she felt she needed their friendship the most. She felt they let her down. She found out later in life that it was their parents who forbade them to hang around her; it was not their choice. She guessed that their parents thought that her being pregnant at the age of thirteen would somehow rub off on them, as if it was contagious.

Tina forgave herself for introducing her best friend (Tammy) to her uncle (Triston). The two later became a couple. She saw that they were quickly falling in love with each other. Eventually, her uncle introduced Tammy to crack cocaine, which sent them both spiraling out of control. She felt helpless because she couldn't stop them. Then she got angry because she knew that they knew better and were smarter than that. Their addiction was what drove a wedge between Tammy and Tina. Later in life, Tina learned that Tammy found God, got clean, and stayed clean. Tammy still had her struggles, but she knew who she could turn to when she needed help.

Tina forgave the paternal cousin (Billy Dukes) of her maternal cousin (Christina Hash) for taking her analginity. Billy came to Phoenix, Arizona, to stay with his cousin Christina for the summer to see if he wanted to relocate there. Tina stayed over one Saturday night to babysit her cousin's kids (including her own daughter Keyla) while they went out to a club. Billy came home earlier than Christina so that he could zone in on her. Tina and the kids were fast asleep. She woke to him licking and putting hickeys on her inner thighs, which was painful. He then pushed her shorts to the side and begin to perform oral sex on her, which was her first encounter with that. She was very intrigued. He talked her into going upstairs in an empty room, next to the room where the kids were sleeping, to have sex. He began to have sex with her from the back and slipped his penis into the wrong hole. Tina was upset and scared because it was very painful, she was bleeding bad, and he wouldn't stop, even though she begged him to, until he exploded inside of her. She believed that he did that on purpose. The next morning, she and her daughter went home. She didn't say anything about what had transpired. Billy left Phoenix never to visit his cousin Christina again.

Tina forgave her ex-boyfriend (Fisher Gain) for accusing her of giving him gonorrhea. They dated for a short period of time. He came to her one day telling her that she gave him an STD. She knew she didn't give him an STD because she was faithful to him. So she knew that he was out fooling around. She went to the nearest health department to get checked out. She went through the embarrassment of having a medical instrument scrape the inside of her vagina, only to find that she did not have gonorrhea or any other disease. She confronted Fisher and showed him her test results. He said that he was very sorry and he knew where he had gotten it from. Tina broke up with him on the spot; they remained friends without benefits.

Tina forgave Wendell Raynor for making her hide in the closet of his room. She had to hide there because his mom was prejudiced and didn't like black people. She couldn't know that her white son was sleeping with a black girl. Tina was very angry stuck in that closet for an hour. Wendell's mom finally left to go back to work, and Tina was free to come out. She made him take her home, and they argued the entire way. She couldn't understand why he didn't just tell his mom who she was or introduce her. Tina never got a chance to meet his mom but did meet his younger brother. She figured she wasn't good enough for him to take home to meet his mom. Their relationship didn't last much longer after that encounter. She did miss riding in his sports car, which was orange with black stripes on the top of the hood.

Tina forgave her second child's father (Frank) for avoiding his responsibility. He got more than he bargained for from their one-night stand. He chose to run and not be a part of his son's life. They later in life met and began to build a relationship. It took a paternity test before they could get to that point. Their son was elated that the paternity test came back 99.9 percent that he was indeed his father. Tina already knew he was the father.

Tina forgave herself for blaming her second child (Donovan) for, as she felt, almost getting her kicked out of her parent's house onto the streets when she was pregnant with him. She thought that he should have been able to sense from the womb that if her stepfather found out that he was in there, he would evict them and his sister (Keyla). She expected her unborn son to not grow so fast, which made her stomach protrude. That was the day all hell broke loose, when her stepfather noticed. She believed and was hoping that she could get away with hiding her pregnancy, which did not work.

Tina forgave herself for even thinking of committing suicide over a guy. Her ex-boyfriend (Hakeem), whom she wanted to be her second child's father, broke up with her after finding out that her baby was his cousin's (Frank). Because this was the first guy whom she loved (outside of her cousin Jersey, which didn't count), she was devastated. She had made plans one day after school to walk to the nearest park, jump in the lake (even though she couldn't swim) and chill with the alligators. She stood at the edge of the lake and talked to God instead. She eventually got over him and that day.

Tina forgave a boy (Don Smith) that she liked for allowing his friend (Mark Status) to have sex with her too. Tina met Don at an abandoned apartment to have sex with him and him only. When he and she were done having sex, his friend Mark pushed Tina back down on the rug and got on top of her. Don watched Mark go into her, and he didn't say or do anything to stop it. Tina didn't give him permission to do this to her, and she even told him no. He ignored her and kept on going until he was beginning to reach his climax. He then jumped up to avoid any of his sperm getting inside of her. Tina was very angry with them both. She just walked away and put in her mind that the incident never took place. It was obvious that Don didn't like her, and it was a setup. This was her first taste of what Snoop Dogg's song "Ain't No Fun (If the Homies Can't Have None)" meant.

Tina forgave herself for liking Webster (who was a virgin at the time and really liked her too) but sleeping with his older brother (Sean). She didn't mean to do it; it just happened. She went over to their house one day to hang out with her best friend (Rhonda) and see her beau (Webster), but they were not home. Sean was there, so she decided to sit and wait for the others to come back home. Sean went into the room that he shared with Webster. Tina followed to see what he was doing. He was looking through sports magazines, and she joined him. For some odd reason, they ended up in the top bunk of the bunk bed, which was his, having sex. She later told Rhonda about it, but she wasn't sure if Webster ever found out about it or not. They all carried on with life like it never took place.

She forgave the four guys (Lance Wild, Ray Law, Bruce Joy, and Larry Wallace) who offered her a ride home one night after a party but made a detour. Tina was at a party and had just been caught by Webster kissing his best friend Wendell, who was the guy that her best friend Rhonda liked, outside at the back of the building. Her guilt lured her into getting drunk and wanting to go home before her original ride was ready to leave. Lance offered her a ride home, and she took it and got into the backseat because she knew him and the other guys in the car. She had no reason to think that they would try anything inappropriate with her. On the way home, Lance pulled into a parking lot in front of a recreation center and parked the car. Three of the guys took advantage of Tina one by one while she was drunk in the backseat of the car. Lance was the driver and apparently the lookout. Ray and Bruce were successful in having her, but Larry was not, due to being too large. When they were done with her, they took her home and didn't look back to see if she even made it in the house or not. After that night, Tina always wondered why Lance didn't just drive her straight home like a Good Samaritan. She also wondered why he didn't try her like the others. Out of guilt and shame, she didn't bother to report the incident. Besides, it would have been their word against hers.

Tina forgave herself for mimicking what her stepfather had done to her to her female cousin (Nima Flash). She was seventeen at that time, and her cousin was fifteen. They were in her cousin's room roughhousing, and amid a flip, Tina looked down inside of the front of her cousin's jeans. She apologized to her cousin, but her cousin didn't seem to mind what had happened. However, Tina felt disgusted with herself and vowed never to do anything like that ever again, which she didn't. She left that day wondering if she had scarred her cousin's mind like her mind was scarred by her stepfather.

Tina forgave Gary Rogue for trying to force himself on her one day while she was on her way to the corner store. Tina used to take a shortcut to the corner store, which was a path through the backyard of two homes. She was walking through the path to get her mom some peach snuff from the store, and Gary jumped out from behind the bushes. Gary was tall, big, and strong. He grabbed her, throwing her down to the ground and began to grind hard on top of her. He attempted to take off her clothes, but one of the neighbors saw and yelled for him to leave her alone. That scared him, so he got up off her and walked away. Tina went on to the store and bought what she was told to.

She then took the long way back home. No more shortcuts for her. She didn't bother to mention it to her mom because she didn't think she would believe her. She later heard that Gary was trying to grab any vulnerable young girl that took that shortcut. She wasn't sure if he ever was reported or if someone beat him down for messing with their daughter, sister, niece, etc.

Tina forgave Mack Rogue for forcing himself on her one evening, in Granada Park. They were joy riding in his station wagon, and he parked it in the park near a wooded area. They moved to the wagon part (back/trunk) of the station wagon for comfort. They talked, laughed, and played around a little until Mack began to get frisky. Tina told him to calm down, but he became more aggressive. She then told him to stop, but he kept going. He didn't stop until her panties were pulled to the side and he was inside of her. She still was telling him no and to stop, which he did, after he was done. She got out of the back of the car, not uttering a word. She got into the passenger's sit and waited for him to drive her back home. He was a mechanic and it was a long time before she got that oil smell out of her senses. She never saw or spoke to him again. That was another event that she would carry to her grave. She began to believe that maybe she had asked for what happened to her.

Tina forgave her relatives (Olivia and Morris Grant) for at first taking her son Donovan from her, without her permission, as if she was an unfit mother. She considered that to be kidnapping and could have pressed charges. They took her son because her cousin Nima, who was babysitting him at the time, overheard her talking to Raven's aunt. They were making plans for her aunt to raise Tina's son until he was five years old, which would have allowed Tina time to get on her feet. Nima called her relatives, and they came and took Donovan while she was walking to the grocery store. When she got back to her apartment, her son was gone and so was her cousin, so she knew something was up. She found out from her cousin where her son was and thought about everything for a minute. She figured she would have fun (rip and run the streets whenever she had a babysitter for her daughter) for at least two weeks and then go get her son. When she went back to get her son, they gave him to her with just the clothes on his back. They were going to teach her for taking him back, knowing that she really had no means to care for him.

Tina forgave her mom for calling her stupid at a point in her life when she needed her the most. Tina had gotten Donovan back from her relatives. She had hope that she could take care of his sister Keyla and him on her own. Her relatives turned him over to her with only the clothes on his back. Tina needed pampers for Donovan, so she asked her mom for money to get them. Her mom gave her the money but called her stupid for getting her son back, knowing that she couldn't take care of both kids at that time in her life. She eventually found it to be too difficult and allowed her relatives to pick Donovan up. Tina vowed never to come and get him again, but if he wanted to come live with her in his teenage years, she wouldn't stop him. Hence, that was why Tina did not like to use or hear the word stupid ever again.

Tina forgave her third child's father (Steve) for dodging his responsibility by running off and getting married. She later found out that that relationship ended up being a lie. She was mad at him for a little while because he didn't want to give his son his last name. Steve and Tina were messing around with each other on and off. She eventually figured out that he was only with her to get her to take him off child support. He really didn't love her like he claimed.

81

Tina forgave her ex-boyfriend (John Brooke) for the times that he was violent with her. The first time he was violent with her was when they were at this little corner hangout spot, and he saw her there with her cousin (Missy Ham). This was not a place where she'd normally hang out. He knew it and was furious. He walked over to her, grabbed her shoulders, and began to shake her violently. He then pushed her up against the car and told her to go home. Because she had never seen him act this way before and it scared her, she drove home just as he demanded. She was thinking that he was up to no good and just didn't want her to see what he was doing.

The second time John was violent with her was when they were at her apartment (in the projects) and they got into an argument over him cheating. Tina said, "I can cheat too if that's the game you want to play." John was not happy with her reply. He pushed her down onto the couch, took his fist and smooshed it into the crown of her head (so as not to leave marks) repeatedly until he got tired. Still angry at her, he picked up the coffee table and threw it into the front-room window of the apartment. He walked out of her apartment quickly because he knew that the police would be there soon. Sure enough, one of her neighbors called the police. The police wrote up a report based on the information that Tina had given them, but they couldn't find John anywhere. She later found out that he had caught the city bus home. She had to pay for the window to be fixed out of her own pocket, and he didn't contribute one dime, even though he was the one who broke it.

The third time John was violent with her was when he, she, her best friend Belinda, and Belinda's boyfriend at the time, Max Black, were at a club in Phoenix called Bahabreeze. Tina was wearing a tight mustard-colored dress that fit her body well. John was loving that his woman was looking fly until he noticed other guys were looking at her and trying to talk to her. She and Belinda sat down in a lounge area over near the wall. He and Max walked around checking out the rest of the club, drinks in hand, leaving Belinda and her alone to chat. When they came back, Max and Belinda went on the dance floor to dance. John felt that Tina was looking a little too sexy. So he decided to flip the chair that she was sitting in over with her still sitting on it. That caused her to hit her head on the stone wall behind the chair. She was crying, hurt, humiliated, and ready to go home. Max and Belinda saw what had happened and were a little uneasy about the whole situation. As they were leaving the club, heading back to her car, John decided that he was not finished humiliating Tina. He then went to hit her with a closed fist, and Max stopped him right in his tracks. Max was much shorter than John but more muscular. Max picked John up off the ground, with one hand around his neck. He told him, "You will never hit a woman around me, ever," and dropped him down to the ground. Tina was not sure how John got home, but he didn't ride back with them. She was low-key happy inside because Max had stood up for her. She always had great respect for him for that. Also, she saw John for the coward that he was. He wanted to fight her but not a man. Unfortunately, Tina was not completely done with John just yet. Let her tell it – she was in love, and her love could change him.

The fourth time John got violent with Tina was when she decided to surprise him at his house, which he and his roommate shared. She had been there many times before and figured it would be no problem just to pop in. She was wrong that evening. She drove there with her cousin Missy. Her plan was to let him know how much she'd missed him. She wanted to show him sexually. When she got there, she rang the doorbell, and his roommate came to the door saying, "John isn't there." Tina didn't buy that story one bit because his car was there and his room light was on. She wasn't going to leave until he came to the door. John finally came to the door to say, "I'm sick with a headache and I don't want any company. I'm going to turn in early." Out of the corner of her eye, she saw a girl walk from the bathroom to his room. She then attempted to push the door open so that she could get a clear understanding of who the girl was and who she was with. John used all his might to keep Tina from getting in. He knew that he was busted cheating. He grabbed her car keys from her hand and threw them out on the ground, toward her car. As soon as she bent over to pick them up, he lightly kicked her on the butt, which plunged her forward toward her car door. He then grabbed her by the seat of her pants and the top of her shirt and tried to throw her in the car. She hit her head on the top of the car, where the driver-side door meets when it's closed. At that point, she was hurt and just wanted to leave, which she did. All the while, her cousin Missy was yelling at him to stop and, of course, laughing as well. Tina recalls nothing funny about that night.

The last time that John was violent with her was when she decided to break up with him. He seemed to be on board at first. John asked her to please give him a ride to the main bus terminal in Phoenix. She agreed, but she had her best friend Rhonda ride with her, just in case he started to act crazy. Once Tina got John closer to the bus terminal, he cursed her out. She cursed him out too. He then took the car gear and yanked it into park, to damage her car. As he was getting out of the car, he began to kick her on the side of her body, anywhere where his size thirteen shoe could fit. Everyone at the bus terminal and on the bus that had just pulled in could see what he had done. Rhonda didn't say or do anything; it was obvious that she was shocked and scared. Tina was embarrassed, scared, and officially done with him. She soon found out that the reason John had gone from a good guy to bad guy was that he had begun snorting cocaine.

Tina forgave herself for leaving her kids at home when they were younger to go to the club down the street. She felt that she was missing something, like her teenage/young adulthood. Because her kids were fed, bathed, and gone to sleep, everything would be okay. She also thought that because she was going back and forth checking on them, all was well. When she was running back home to check on them, she would think, what if the apartment caught on fire? She would even think, what if someone was watching her leave and broke in and harmed her kids? She even went as far as to think, what if someone called child protective services on her? She couldn't enjoy herself while at the club for worrying so much, so she finally chose to get a babysitter or not go out.

Tina forgave herself for going to the club down the street one night, approaching a man that she knew (Eugene Crow, the DJ) and telling him that she wanted to see what he was all about. She could not believe what she had done. They'd flirted with each other several times before, but that's as far as it went since he thought she was underage. Once he found out that she was a young adult, he was so intrigued by her directness, aggressiveness, and know-what-I-want attitude that he obliged her with no hesitation. That made her feel special because all the women wanted him and couldn't have him. He was so handsome, fine (he was a que dog with his fraternity's brands on his arms and torso) and had those big dreamy green eyes. After the club closed, she got nervous and wanted to call it off. She didn't know what she was going to do with this hunk of a man. She didn't want to appear as a teaser or inexperienced sexually. She told herself that she had to follow through with what she had started. He drove her back to her apartment (in the projects) and had his way with her. He

85

showed her exactly what he was all about, which was more than she bargained for. She was mesmerized and wanted to have more of him, but all to herself. They had sex only one more time after that, maybe a week later, because she discovered that he had a girlfriend. She would have been the side chick, had she continued.

Tina forgave herself for sleeping with a man (Judas Freeman), who was older than her parents, for money to pay her electric bill. At least, that's what she told the man. She didn't really need the money but was being greedy. Other women she knew (relatives and friends) made sleeping with men for money look like a way to live lavishly. She had the money to pay her electric bill but wanted extra cash to buy herself something nice. She thought that this would be their little secret and maybe he could be her sugar daddy, but boy, was she wrong. He was a handsome old man, which made it a little easier for her to go through with it. One day he came over to her apartment, paid her the money that she had asked for earlier that week when she saw him driving down the street and stopped him, and slept with her. They started in her room with him caressing her breast. They ended up in the bathroom with her bent over the toilet, holding onto the lid on the back of it as he pounded away. Even though it was quick, as soon as they finished doing the do, he walked down the street to what the neighborhood called the gossip apartment and told everyone who was sitting on the front porch that day. Tina felt so low and grimy. Her maternal uncle (Clarence Slogan) was sitting on that porch and heard that old man telling all her business. He walked down to her apartment, knocked on the door, and told her what was just said. Tina tried to lie to him, but he knew she was lying because she began to cry. He told her, "Never do anything like that again. If you need anything, come to me." She was so embarrassed and ashamed, but what he said was etched in her brain forever. She never did anything like that again with any man, young or old. She had heard the old folks say once, "If you have sex with an old man, you'll get worms." Even though she knew that it was probably a myth, she found herself in the bathroom examining her vagina with a hand-held mirror. Everything appeared to be/look okay down there, and boy, was she relieved.

Tina forgave her ex-boyfriend (Lee Morse), whom she met when she was in the police academy, for giving her genital herpes. A year into their relationship, she began to break out with small sores on the inner lips of her vagina. She told Lee about it, and he kissed her and gave her a hug. She thought that was a bit odd that he didn't get angry with her or question her at all. Most guys would have been upset about the situation. Instead, he bought some betadine swabs from the drug store, took her to her apartment, and nursed her wounds. Tina eventually went to the doctor to get tested and was diagnosed with having genital herpes. The doctor prescribed her medication to help ease her discomfort. Through her tears and hyperventilating, she showed Lee the test results, and he said that everything would be okay since they were going to be together forever. She couldn't believe that he had knowingly given her a sexually transmitted disease (STD). She couldn't trust him anymore after that.

Tina decided that her world was truly over, and she was going to end it by taking the bottle of pills that she was prescribed by her doctor. Surely, she couldn't tell anyone else that she had an STD. She took the pills, went to sleep, and woke up with a bad stomachache and headache. She thanked God for her life, asked for forgiveness and then forgave herself.

Tina later forgave herself for committing to a threesome to keep her relationship with Lee together. The threesome included his ex-girlfriend. They were all at his apartment one day, and Tina pretty much watched her boyfriend have sex with another woman. She remembered feeling angry because she couldn't stand the sight of seeing the man that she loved screwing someone else. When it was her turn, she didn't even want him to touch her. Once it was all over, he was very happy, of course, but Tina began to look at him differently. At this point, their relationship was going downhill fast. Tina's mind began to play tricks on her. She was wondering if her boyfriend and his ex were meeting up to have sex privately after that incident took place. She learned never to invite anyone else into her relationship/bed, especially to hold onto a man. She felt that if Lee really loved her, he wouldn't have asked for a threesome in the first place.

Tina forgave herself for judging a book by its cover with her friend's two teenage boys. She met Sabrina Fox at the police precinct where she worked. Sabrina worked in the front office as a secretary, which was how she and Tina became good friends. Tina stayed over at Sabrina's apartment one Saturday night because they were going out to a club. She had shown Sabrina a forest-green Timberland long-sleeve shirt that she was going to wear with some jeans. They both were going to dress casually that night. Later, about two hours before they were to leave, Tina's shirt was missing. Sabrina knew she had it because Tina had shown it to her earlier that day. One of Sabrina's sons looked and dressed like a thug but was respectful. He had also been in and out of the juvenile detention center. Her other son looked and dressed like a well-educated schoolboy, was well-mannered, respectful, and stayed out of trouble. In Tina's mind, she'd already accused the boy who looked like a thug of stealing her shirt. It turned out to be his brother (the one that looked innocent) who stole her shirt. His mom made him give it back to Tina and made him apologize to her as well. She just couldn't believe what she had witnessed.

Tina forgave her fourth child's father (Jerome) for ditching his responsibility by choosing the streets over his child. She knew that he didn't want to be inundated with the woes of fatherhood. She knew he had two other women pregnant, and he probably wasn't going to take care of their children either. This was one of the excuses she used to do what she did. She felt that he should have been there to comfort her after the fact, but he was too busy enjoying the streets.

Tina forgave herself for taking a pill that may have contributed to the miscarriage of her fourth child. She felt like she was pushed into a corner and had no choice. She didn't believe that she could handle having another child alone. Regardless of her excuses, she shouldn't have done it. After the fact, she wondered if the baby would have been a boy or girl. Whenever she saw Jerome's other kids, she wondered if her baby would have looked like any of them.

Tina chose to forgive her oldest brother, Darrius, for not protecting her, due to ripping and running the streets, trying to be Phoenix's next kingpin. He was well known and an ostentatious dresser. He had connections everywhere and a certain street power. She felt that he should have shown her the ropes to this thing called life and the streets. He could have prevented her from going through half of the things that she went through, dealing with men and the street game. Instead, she had to learn and figure it all out on her own. She felt that he was a very selfish individual, but she loved him.

Tina forgave herself for selling a piece of crack to her friend (Rita Garcia) once. She found it on the floor of her apartment when she lived in the projects. That let her know that her brother Darrius had been there that day while she was gone. She felt that she had to get rid of it quickly but didn't want to just throw it away. Her friend Rita came by looking for her brother, but she explained to her that he wasn't there. She asked Rita, "What do you want my brother for?" Rita told her, and Tina gave her what she found on her floor. Rita compensated her for it and walked away. Tina's guilt weighed heavily on her mind. The next time she saw Rita, she apologized to her. Rita accepted her apology, they hugged each other and were on their merry way. Tina was very proud of Rita because she eventually kicked her habit and became an upstanding citizen of their community.

Tina forgave herself for trying to be like her oldest brother. She gave someone whom she trusted her rent money to purchase product. Her aim was to flip the money, but she never got the chance. Once she got the product in hand and attempted to sell it, she was robbed. She lost everything and became furious. She told Darrius what had happened, hoping that he would confront the man who robbed her and put him in his place. Instead, he just laughed at her and told her, "You had no business trying to sell anything, especially when you don't know what you're doing." Tina never got involved with that lifestyle ever again, not to mention she was a month behind on her rent. She had to pay her normal rent and an extra one hundred dollars a month until she caught up.

Tina forgave herself for knowingly messing around with a married man. She knew that her third baby's father (Steve) was married when she slept with him later in life, but he claimed that they were separated. She believed that because she didn't cause their separation, she was doing nothing wrong. She thought that he would eventually divorce his wife for her. Tina found that he was done with his wife, but she wasn't done with him yet. His wife harassed them both. Tina was getting tired of the drama, and her conscience began to convict her. She knew she was wrong on all levels, and she apologized to his wife. They both eventually broke off the facade and went on with their separate lives.

Tina forgave her fifth child's father (Puma) for not sticking around for his responsibility. She figured he was too inebriated off his own lies, that he couldn't stay around even if he wanted to. The fairytale that he sold to her was quickly unraveling. She didn't want her son to be a part of the foolery, but he began to see what was happening as he grew older. He saw that love was not winning between his mother and father. Tina was glad that Puma finally allowed their son to meet his other sisters. She explained to Puma how important it was for them to meet so that they didn't end up meeting somewhere else, like in another state, and begin dating each other. That would be a disaster.

Tina chose to forgive her best friend (Belinda) for approaching her then-fiancé Puma, letting him know that he could come to her if he needed someone to talk to. Puma told Tina, because it made him feel very uncomfortable. He told her that Belinda came at him in a seductive, sexual manner. She believed him and confronted her but was told that she meant no harm by it. Tina couldn't believe that Belinda would even do something like that. She kept her eye on Belinda after that.

Tina forgave herself for unknowingly messing around with a married man. Once she found out that her fifth baby's father (Puma) was in fact married, Tina didn't let go of him right away. She loved him and couldn't just turn it off so quickly. She continued to sleep with him in hopes that he would marry her as he had promised. After all, he had gotten down on one knee and proposed to her. A part of her was hoping that because she had his first and only son, he would divorce his wife and stay. She vowed from that day to never mess with a married man again.

Tina forgave her best friend (David Leach) for not keeping in touch as a true best friend would. He got married and appeared to fall off the face of the earth. He missed her very important life events like graduations, deaths in the family, etc. She understood that once a person got married, their spouse became their best friend. That didn't mean you totally walk away from earlier friends. They had always been there for each other. She thought that maybe he walked away because they crossed the line once. After that, they both decided that they were better off as friends, and that's how they kept it. Perhaps he still thought that Tina wanted him in some way, but she truly didn't.

Tina chose to forgive her friend (Shamya Turner), whom she met at the police academy, for ending their ten-year friendship over money she borrowed. Shamya was going through a personal hardship at that time and needed money to get out of it. Because they were good friends, Tina offered to lend her the large amount of money she needed. She told her that she had to pull the money from her credit card but would need it back as soon as possible. Shamya assured Tina that she would pay it back as soon as she could. She did pay Tina back half of the money, but then she stopped calling her. She started acting strange (mean and rude) and soon disconnected her phone. Tina was in a situation where she needed the rest of her money to pay her own bills, so she decided to ask Shamya for her money back. She knew where she lived and drove to her house to talk to her. She saw her look out of the window and close the blinds, so she left her a note. She never heard from her again and considered the lost money water under the bridge. Tina learned to be very leery of who she let borrow money and who she called a friend in the future. Had she known that lending Shamya money was going to end their friendship, she wouldn't have done it. She preferred their friendship instead.

Tina forgave herself for allowing her relatives (Olivia and Morris) to raise her oldest son (Donovan) from one year old until adulthood. They didn't have any kids at that time. She thought that she was doing a great thing by allowing this. She thought that it would be good for at least one of her kids to be raised in a two-parent household. Instead, her son was mentally, verbally, and emotionally abused. She couldn't understand how Olivia could be so mean and negative. Tina didn't realize it until her son was an adult and begin to voice his pain and resentment.

Tina was blessed that her relatives had seen fit for her, her son, and his siblings to be in each other's lives on a regular basis. That helped make their bonds a little stronger. Once her son became an adult, he began to spend more time with Tina and his siblings, but she was sure that he had some resentment toward her. He might have felt abandoned by both of his biological parents. If she could do things over again, she would have kept her son home with her and his siblings. She hoped that one day her son would seek counseling so that he could begin to heal from any internal scars that he might have. Tina's son was somewhat of a loner, as she was. He didn't come around the family as much as she'd like. She never bothered him about it; she just let him come around whenever he felt like it. Whenever he came around, the entire family always enjoyed his company and presence.

Tina forgave herself for propositioning her best friend (Raven) to participate in a foursome, them and two guys. Her best friend said, "Heck, no!" She then stated, "I'm flattered, but I'm not with that." Tina profusely apologized, and they never visited that conversation again during their friendship. She thought that their friendship would have been awkward after that, but it wasn't. Raven knew that Tina was embarrassed and meant no harm. She also knew that Tina knew not to raise that question again.

Tina forgave her daughter (Keyla) for running away from home when she was around sixteen. She ran away because she was placed on a punishment for the entire summer for bringing home bad grades. Tina whooped Keyla with a belt for her bad grades, and her daughter looked at her like, Mom, that doesn't work anymore. That was Keyla's last whooping. She waited until her mom was sleep and snuck out of the back door. She walked over to her aunt's apartment and began to live there. Tina knew where her daughter was and called the police to have her escorted back home. The police told Tina that there was nothing that they could do because Keyla was sixteen and Tina knew where she was. Tina left her daughter there, went home and cried herself to sleep. She spent the next two weeks worrying about her and praying for her. She would see Keyla out driving her aunt's car like she had no cares in the world. Tina had gotten to the point where she let go and let God.

She told Keyla to come and get all her belongings and take them over to her aunt's apartment. When the summer was over, Keyla came back home with apologies on board, just in time for school to start. Tina found out that Keyla was liking some little boy and was no longer a virgin. So she made sure that she was put on birth control pills. Tina told her that if she ran away again, she would not be coming back to her house.

Tina forgave herself for jumping on her flip-mouthed son (Martin) in front of her mom, with no regard for her mother. They were over to her mom's house and had just finished eating dinner. Tina told her son to go outside and play with his other siblings. He said to her, "You make me sick!" She was standing in the kitchen, and he was in the family room.

She asked him, "What did you say?" Tina knew that most kids would have said, "I didn't say nothing." Not her son! Her son repeated the very same words over again, in the same order. She leaped over on him like she was Floyd Mayweather. She soon forgot where she was. She then faintly heard in the background her mom telling her, "Take that mess outside and don't tear up my fake plant and whatnots." Her bumping her hip against her youngest son's (Demetrius) head, which hit the stool as she was dragging Martin out of the door, was what stopped her in her tracks. After she put Martin in his place, she quickly apologized to her mom for disrespecting her house and both sons for what had just taken place.

Tina forgave herself for one day grabbing her son Martin around the neck. She saw that he was having a problem with completing his chores. She didn't like repeating herself nor did she tolerate a flip-mouthed child. That day, he voiced to her that he didn't feel like washing the dishes and wanted to just chill in his room. She asked him a total of three times to do the dishes and got no response from him nor any movement. She then walked over to his room door, and he began mouthing off to her. Before she knew it, she blacked out. When she came back to, she was straddling him with her hand around his neck, telling him to be quiet and not to say another word. Tina didn't remember much about that event, because, according to her son, he had to kick her off him. She found that very hard to believe because had he kicked her, she probably would have been incarcerated for beating him to a pulp. Her son washed the dishes, and they didn't have any more issues around chores after that.

Tina forgave herself for putting her son Martin out of the house at thirteen years old. She was very strict and didn't have much time for nonsense. She had allowed him to hang out at his friend's house that day but had already told him that he could not stay overnight. He insisted on calling and annoying her until he thought he was going to get his way. Later that night, he called back, and she didn't answer the phone. Martin was talking smack about his mom to his friend's mom but didn't realize the conversation was being recorded on his mom's answering service. Tina listened to the message and became enraged at the disrespect. She told his friend's mom to come and get his belongings so that he could live with her, being that he wanted to be grown. Martin thought that his mom was joking but soon found out that she wasn't. They came to get his clothes and off they went. Tina was serious about her son not coming back home, even though she was worried about him and missed him. She just wasn't going to have a disrespectful kid living in her home. A week later, after he came to his senses and apologized, he was welcomed back home with open arms.

Tina forgave her daughter (Keyla) for damaging the engine on her brand new, 2006 Lexus IS250. She damaged the engine by racing Tina's car on a speedway racing track with her friends. She left her car with her daughter to drive, with respect and care, while she was out of town. While she was away, she received a call from Keyla stating that the car was making a weird noise. Tina asked her, "Why is the car making noise?"

Keyla replied, "The car wash person jerked the car vigorously." Tina waited until she got back home to deal with the matter. Once she got back home, Tina took the car to the dealership to see what was wrong with it and found that the engine was damaged. She was told that it was the pistons and other things. She was told that normal daily wear and tear of a manual transmission car should not have caused that much damage to her car. They wanted to charge her full price to fix the engine because it was considered the operator's error that the engine was damaged. Tina was angry since she had only had the car for three months. She couldn't afford to get it fixed, so she was forced to sell it. Her daughter Keyla assisted her in getting the car sold as soon as possible. A month later, Tina's mom told her that Keyla did, in fact, race her car that weekend, when she went out of town. Tina allowed Keyla to still live and she eventually got another new vehicle.

Tina forgave her ex-boyfriend (Carter Ransom) for the times he was violent with her. The first time he was violent with her was when she wanted to end their very short relationship, but he was not having it. She was helping him clear out the dresser drawer that she had allotted him. He felt that he didn't need her help and pulled her arm as hard as he could, which jerked her entire body across the floor, away from the dresser. She looked at him strangely, wondering what just happened. Carter apologized to her, and they quickly made up. They both put his clothes back in the dresser drawer. However, Tina kept that incident in the back of her mind.

The second time that Carter got violent with her was when Tina wouldn't do what he told her to do. He was a bit of a controller, and she was not to be controlled. He then kicked over one of her end tables, which had a display of whatnots and candles on it. The end table did not break, but everything that was on it shattered once it hit the floor. Fortunately, her kids were outside playing and didn't hear any of the commotion. Tina could tell by the look on his face that he knew he had messed up by kicking over her end table. All Tina could think about was, would that be her the next time? He turned the end table back upright and put it back in its place. He then grabbed the broom and dustpan to clean up the mess he'd made. He began to apologize to her profusely. She still stayed in a relationship with him, thinking that he had been through a lot and needed someone to love him.

Carter began to stalk and threaten Tina because she no longer wanted to be with him. He started stalking her by walking behind the neighbors' houses to get to her house without her seeing him coming. He didn't want her family to see him coming either because they would have warned her via phone call or beat him up. When Carter rang the doorbell, Tina yelled out, "I'm calling the police!" He left her house the same way he came, behind the neighbors' houses. She didn't call the police but should have.

The third time Carter was violent with Tina was when he rode his bike over twenty miles to her house so that he could catch her as she was going to work one morning. She was getting ready to get in the car when he came from behind a mini palm tree that was in front of her house, near the left side of the house, which was a blind spot for her. He came up behind her with a knife, which scared her half to death. That let her know that she was really dealing with a psycho. Carter demanded that she take him and his bike back to his home. She played along by telling him that she loved him. She then told him, "If I didn't have a meeting as soon as I get to work, I would take you." She told him, "We can talk about things later." He kissed her on the lips, got on his bike, and rode off. She was shaken up but still managed to go to work that day and didn't get the police involved.

Carter did not hear back from Tina. So he decided to pop up at her job as she was getting off from work. It was pouring down rain. She couldn't see where he had come from or figure out how he got there. He scared her again by catching her off guard. As soon as she put the key in the ignition, he was banging on the passenger's side window, wanting her to let him in. She first refused but then let him into the car. She figured once they got back to her house, she could end this relationship once and for all. While they sat in Tina's family room, she told Carter that their relationship was really over this time. She could no longer deal with his controlling nature. He became enraged and told her, "I'm gonna harm your kids."

Tina walked to her room, wrote "Go over to your grandma's house" on a sheet of printer paper with a black sharpie marker, walked to her kids' rooms and showed it to them. They rapidly followed the instruction. Once Tina saw that they were out of the house and safe, she looked Carter in the eyes and told him, "I'm no longer afraid of you." He thought that he was going to make her afraid of him again by making her drive him wherever he wanted to go. She agreed, just to get him out of her house so that she could lock the door. She told him, "I'm going across the street to my parents' house to use the phone." He thought that she was calling the police on him, so he left her house walking fast. She really wasn't calling the police, but her plan worked. She knew he had just gotten out of prison and didn't want to go back. Tina had originally started dating him only because he claimed to know her oldest brother Darrius. He was handsome and fine. It turned out Darrius didn't know Carter at all. Tina never saw Carter again after that day.

Tina forgave herself for judging her son-in-law's motives regarding her daughter, which were based on her own past experiences. Because she knew that karma was real, she wanted them to do things the right way. In her eyes, the right way was to close one chapter before opening another. Once the forbidden barrier was crossed, she didn't want her son-in-law with her daughter. She felt that Keyla could do better. She knew that the world knew how they had gotten together and that their lives would be scrutinized. She felt that their relationship would be cursed because they didn't have a sturdy foundation. She believed that he would break her daughter's heart into a million pieces. She then began to see God at work in their lives and again was shown that He could fix anything if she just prayed and believed. Her son-in-law turned out to have a kind spirit after all, and Tina welcomed her into their family.

Tina forgave herself for losing the land that her real father (Lifeline) transferred to her before he was sent to prison. She had it for two years and paid the taxes on it. She eventually had a three-bedroom, two-bath house built on the land. She and her kids lived in their new home for ten years before it was put into foreclosure. It was put into foreclosure because of Tina's greed. She refinanced her home twice to pay off or pay down debt, which she managed to run back up. Based on the rules and regulations dealing with refinancing, she was not qualified to refinance once, let alone twice. Over time, the refinancing made her monthly mortgage payment far more than she could afford, and she began to fall behind on her payments. Her falling behind on the mortgage payments sent her into default. After talking to her father and letting him know what was happening, Tina was finally able to short-sale her home, and the mortgage company forgave her the difference. She felt bad because her father had entrusted her with the land in the first place to keep it in the family. Her father had given her the okay and told her to do what she had to do. That helped her to move on, with a valuable lesson learned.

Tina forgave her best friend Rhonda for no longer talking to her and ending their friendship, which really bothered her at first. Rhonda had put her in an awkward predicament by telling her that she had slept with her cousin Chester, Raven's boyfriend of several years. Rhonda chose to call Tina on two occasions to tell her this information. Tina finally chose to speak out on it because it bothered her knowing this information and being in Raven's face with this secret. She knew that once she said something, she could lose one or both friends. She did what she felt was morally right. Rhonda called her a liar, which didn't sit well with Tina. The bottom line was Rhonda slept with Raven's man when she was in a committed relationship with him. Tina at one point felt acrimony toward Rhonda but decided to let it go as not to contaminate her soul.

What Tina didn't get was why did Rhonda choose this incident to get so mad at her about when they had been through far worse. She knew it couldn't have been about loyalty because if that were the case, Rhonda's loyalty card would have been revoked a long time ago. They'd been through cheating scandals, threesomes (which Tina was supposed to just watch from inside the closet), being busted for stealing jeans out of a store when they were younger, swapping driver's licenses, etc. and their friendship stayed intact. As far as the cheating scandals (in which Tina was pursued both times), Tina started them and apologized for them, but Rhonda's fake acceptance of her sincere apology and vengeful heart finished it (by being the pursuer and offering up her services several times).

Tina had a strange ungodly soul tie to Rhonda, which made her question if she was gay or not. She knew she wasn't, because she wasn't attracted to other women in that way. It was just weird for her being around Rhonda. She was at the point where she couldn't care anymore and decided to pray for and love Rhonda from afar. She chose to cherish the good times they'd had and the memories they'd made.

Tina forgave her pastor friend (Akube Mann) for not encouraging her to stay on her celibacy journey. He was more concerned with what he could get from her than her celibacy journey. He was a nice man and appeared to be caring, but she had a gut feeling that he was hiding something. He did stress to her that he was a private person, but he was just too private for her. He claimed not to be married or in a relationship. They only communicated via Facebook inbox for over seven years and met up twice to talk at her apartment but never met anywhere in public. She wondered how many other women he was talking to via Facebook inbox. She began to confide in him and tell him her darkest deepest secrets. They talked about a lot of things over those years. To her, he was like a best friend, and she wanted to hang out with him and get to know him. She became emotionally tied to him. He fed into it by telling her what she wanted to hear, which kept it going. She eventually stopped talking to him because he wasn't who she thought he was. He seemed interested in her in her Facebook inbox, but the last time they hung out and watched Netflix with no chill, his body language displayed that he wasn't interested at all. They both wanted each other sexually, but Tina wanted more (a committed relationship). Akube did not. That was when Tina put her guard back up. She remained celibate but almost let her guard all the way down with him, which could have ended her celibacy journey.

Tina forgave her youngest brother (Liam) for leaving this earth so soon due to heart issues. She knew he was ill, but she didn't know he was that bad off. She thought that he was pretending, just to get more of their mom's attention, until she saw how he was sleeping. She saw that he was having a hard time breathing and would sleep hanging off the side of the bed as if he was praying, when he was at home. Whenever he was in the hospital, she saw that he would sleep sitting up in the lounge chair next to his hospital bed. She saw that those were the only ways he could be comfortable. There were times when the doctors would call Tina's family stating, "Liam only has two to three days left to live" and she/her immediate family would rush to the hospital to be by his side. Then her family was told that he would eventually need a heart transplant. Tina learned that because his heart was so badly damaged from several years of drug and alcohol abuse, he didn't even make it onto the heart transplant list. His death hurt their entire family, especially their mom. Tina saw the changes in her mom and how she missed her baby boy. There were times when she thought her mom was giving up on life. She saw her mom become sad, depressed, and withdrawn. She believed that was the way that her mom grieved. She never saw her mom cry. Perhaps her mom cried when she was alone. Her mom was just never the same after Liam's passing. They all knew that he knew God and rested in knowing that he would be okay until they met again.

Tina forgave her ex-boyfriend (Jerome) for leaving this earth so soon. They had made plans to try a relationship again, for the one-hundredth time. She was confident that this time it was going to work because she prayed about it. They prayed for each other. He was supposed to move into her new house, and they would live happily ever after. He had gotten himself together and become drug- and alcohol-free. At least that's what he told her. In the past, he had chosen the street life over her, due to his addictions. She was happy that he had a relationship with God and was a God-fearing man. He wasn't perfect, but neither was she. They talked a lot while making their plans via phone, Facebook inbox, and text. They constantly exchanged the words I love you to each other, even though they already knew it.

Tina recalled the last time she saw Jerome, which was one day when they hung out at the park. They were reminiscing about old times and what the future might hold for them. Tina's mom called her cell phone, and she handed the phone over to him. He and her mom were talking and laughing for a while. Her mom remembered him, and she remembered his mom, from back in the day. After talking to her mom, he kissed Tina. Little did she know that would be their last kiss. Not long after that, she heard that Jerome was shot dead. She saw on the news that his murderer was apprehended. His family was relieved. Tina knew that everyone grieved over him that day, especially his kids, his family, and even the many women from his past. She grieved. She didn't understand why God brought them together again, only to take him away from her. Tina found it very ironic that, years ago, he had a roll of bullets tattooed on his arm and then he died by a bullet. Regardless, she loved and missed him tremendously. She wondered if, somehow, he was reunited with their baby that she'd miscarried many years ago.

Tina forgave herself for being impatient with her mom when she was first placed in Hospice care. She wanted her mom to get better and thought that she would if she had just done more. She felt that if her mom had eaten more and drunk more fluids, she would have had more strength to live longer. She felt that if her mom had been a little more mobile, her body wouldn't have given out so quickly. She believed that had she used the bedside commode more, her organs wouldn't have shut down so soon. Tina was hoping that her mom would prove that being put on Hospice care was wrong. She finally realized that when her mom told her that the doctors said there was nothing else that they could do for her, she was serious. The last time she left her mom's side, she knew that would be the last time she saw her alive.

Tina forgave her mom for leaving this earth too soon, due to heart issues. She felt that her mother knew that she had four other kids still here, and they needed her. Her mom was really torn from losing her baby boy. She knew that even though he was a grown man, he was still her mom's baby. Her mom's demeanor was all out of whack. About seven months after her brother's death, her mother had to have minor thyroid surgery. Because her mom had heart problems as well, the surgery was risky. The surgery on her mom didn't go as planned. Her mom could not swallow and, therefore, could not eat or drink. The doctors called Tina's family in to say their goodbyes because her mom was going downhill fast. When they got to the hospital, her family were given the option of letting her mom go or having a feeding tube put into her stomach. Tina's family chose the feeding tube. Eventually, her mom gained back the ability to swallow, which allowed her to drink and eat. A few days later, her mom was released from the hospital. Over the next year, she did have trips back and forth to the hospital, but at least she was still alive. Tina remembered talking to her mom and telling her that, "If there is anyone out there that has hurt you in the past, you would have to forgive them, for God to forgive you."

Her mom said, "I forgive them." Tina knew then that her mom knew God, and she was at peace with that. Soon, her mom's body got weak, and her heart got even weaker. Her mom was turned over to Hospice and made comfortable at home. It was just a matter of time before Tina's mom went to be with her loved ones who had passed before her, especially her baby boy, Liam. Her mom went to sleep for a couple of days and eventually took her last breath. Her whole family was devastated. Her mom was the glue that held the family together. Tina would especially miss the bond they shared, which included them just sitting around sucking their middle two fingers together. They even managed to talk and laugh with their fingers in their mouths. Those were their magical moments. Her mom was gone but would never be forgotten.

Tina forgave her best friends (Rhonda, Belinda, and David) for not reaching out to her when her brother and mom passed away. She could not believe that they didn't reach out to her on the days that the deaths happened or even during the funeral arrangements. She received no call, no text, not even smoke signals. She did hold a grudge for a little while. Eventually, Belinda did reach out to her via text, days after both funerals were over, which Tina acknowledged. She was shocked when Belinda texted her, acknowledging her mom's passing on her birthday. She was like, "Who does that?" She realized that she was grieving and maybe taking things the wrong way, so she let it all go. She thought she heard from Rhonda via text, days after her mom's funeral, but she wasn't sure. She wasn't sure because she didn't remember or recognize her cell phone number. She heard absolutely nothing from David at all. She continued to pray for them all and chose to love them from afar.

Tina forgave God for calling her loved ones home so soon. They all were too young in her opinion. They had more life to live. Her baby brother Liam left behind two kids. Her ex-boyfriend Jerome left behind two kids. Her mom left behind four kids. Her mom was her best friend, so who was she going to talk to now? Who was she going to call up at any time and cry over the phone with now? Who was she going to argue with and then act as if the argument never happened, now that her youngest brother was gone? Who was she going to love and wait on now that her ex-boyfriend was gone? Although she knew that it had to have been their time to go, she wished she could turn back the hands of time.

Tina forgave herself for not being the world's best grandma. She felt that because she became a mother at the age of fourteen, and her kids were now grown, she was done. She loved her grandkids dearly but didn't take them often as most grandmas did. When she wanted to see them and spend time with them, she did. She made sure that their parents picked them up on time, especially if the kids got on her nerves. She would do nice things for them when she had the money, but most of the time she didn't have the means. She loved watching them grow, whether it was in person, via pictures on Facebook/Instagram, or videos. She always wished she could do more for them and be more like what she considered to be a normal grandma, but she couldn't.

Tina forgave herself for not going to church as much as she used to. She had not been to church for several years other than to attend funerals. She came up with excuse after excuse to justify why she hadn't been back. Her first excuse was, the preacher was cheating on his wife. How could she follow someone who was depraved? Her second excuse was, people stared at you too much like, where have you been? Her third excuse was, she cried too much, and it seemed like the pastor's message was always directed right at her. She wasn't a shouter in church; she was a crier. She didn't quite understand that because she wasn't a crier at all outside of church. She felt that she was too strong a woman for that. She didn't have time to be weak or show weakness. She was sure that the churchgoers were wondering why she was crying like that and what she was going through. She later began to attend church again. She came to realize that a person should go to church to hear the word of God, not to judge the person bringing the word. She saw that the pastor was human (not a noman) and made mistakes just like she did. She also learned that going to church was a way of fellowshipping with other believers, which could be a great resource to get her through the week. She realized that crying was her way of cleansing poignant feelings, and everybody went through something, sometime in life. As far as the staring, she was beautiful, so why wouldn't they stare at her?

Tina forgave herself for feeling angry about two relatives that did not attend her mom's funeral. She could not get past their justification as to why they didn't attend.

She heard that one relative did not have enough money to fly home but managed to fly home a week or two later. She heard that the other relative had just started a new job, which she heard nothing else about after that. To Tina, they were just excuses. Tina prayed about the way she felt and decided to continue to love her two relatives from afar.

Tina forgave herself for taking it a little personally that her oldest brother Darrius had not visited her at her new home yet. After all, she had only been living there for five years. Surely, five more years couldn't hurt. She wasn't sure why he had not come to visit yet, but probably he had good reasons. Perhaps, it was too far for him to drive. Not to mention that she had been to visit him about five times since she'd been living there. She figured he would stop by when he got good and ready. Regardless, she loved her brother and always would.

Tina's ability to forgive allowed her to see the grace that God had bestowed upon her. She had to let go of the grudges and ill feelings that she had developed for some of those people who hurt her, as well as herself. She did, over time, by building a relationship with God. She finally understood why she had to forgive. It was to release her from negative energy, which was still giving her transgressors power over her. Forgiveness freed her because she now took that power back.

"For if you forgive others their transgressions, your heavenly Father will also forgive you" (Tree of Life Version, Mat. 6.14).

A Disconnect

There's a disconnect now that my mom is gone, and I'm not quite sure how to feel, a disconnect has caused me to shut down from the world in an effort just to deal.

I'm called the strong one and that I am, for I had to be early in life I swear. With a disconnect even the strong get weak, and when I do cry, there's no shoulder there.

A disconnect has caused me to pray more and read the Word as my mechanism to cope. It's strange how a disconnect could give the one who is disconnected some hope.

Somewhere in a disconnect it will all work out for His good even though I don't see it now, but if I could bring my mom back before she got sick I truly would somehow!

Chapter 6 - God's Grace

≈

Tina credited all her graduations to the grace of God, encouragement from her family and friends, and her zest to succeed. God's grace and mercy were sufficient and saved Tina. His grace was what put all her broken pieces back together again. She didn't die from her life's mishaps. She was still standing. She had a reason to praise God. He turned her test into a testimony and her mess into a message for all to see/hear. His love for her was like no other love. Tina confessed that there were times when she didn't trust God and doubted Him. She thought that because of all the sins she'd committed, He no longer listened to her cries and wouldn't answer her prayers. She felt that He had forsaken her. She quickly learned that He was there all the time, even when she walked away from Him.

In addition to Tina's career and academic experiences, her values and morals were what she considered critical to her success. Her trial and tribulations became more endurable in this cold and wicked world because of her faith in God and His grace, coverage, and deliverance. Because she began to believe that she could do all things through the will of Jesus Christ, she could partially see why her once broken young self could not see past her circumstances. If Tina had been told twenty-nine years ago that she would one day have accomplished all that she has accomplished, she wouldn't have believed it.

Her family also helped her maneuver through this thing called life and kept her going when she no longer wanted to. They were watching her every move. They often told her of the ways that she inspired them to continue their education and offered other life lessons as well. This made Tina feel phenomenal, but she knew it was by God's grace only!

It was God's grace that kept Tina from losing her mind. She'd had gone through a lot, especially during her younger years. What happened to her should have broken her down to the point of being a basket case. It should have taken her to the point of no return, but God had other plans for her life. He took all that bad that was meant to destroy her and turned it into something good. For that alone, Tina was grateful.

God's grace kept Tina alive when doctors said that she could have died, had brain damage, or lost her left eye. She and Darrius use to play Hong Kong Phooey in their front yard when they were younger. There was a cement bench located in the center of the front yard. One day Darrius kicked her a little too hard, which caused her to fall to the ground near the bench. Her body kind of bounced off the ground and the left side of her head landed right on the corner of the cement bench with great force. With so much force, in fact, that all she could see was blackness with a dash of silver shooting through the darkness. Tina saw stars from being knocked senseless. Once she gained her sight back, she began to cry and scream from the excruciating pain. She was also crying because she noticed that there was blood all over her. She remembered asking her mom, "Am I going to die?" Tina's mom grabbed a white towel and held it to her head as she rushed her to the car. Tina's stepfather drove them so fast to the nearest hospital, where they rushed her into surgery. She found out later that she had a gaping hole in the left side of her head (near her temple) and that she was blessed to still be here in the land of the living. She had to have a hundred stitches, fifty on the inside and fifty on the outside, to put her back together again. Fortunately, she didn't die, have brain damage, or lose her left eye. She was released from the hospital a week later to finish recovering at home.

It was God's grace that kept Tina from taking a hit of a laced joint, trying to fit in with two of her friends, who were about that life. She rode her bike to her friend's apartment, in the projects, to meet up with Rhonda. They were smoking, and Tina asked if she could hit the joint that they were smoking. Rita didn't reply, but Rhonda said no. Tina was like, stop playing and trying to be funny. Rhonda told her no again. She then said, this was why I said no. Rhonda pulled out a crack rock, chopped it up, and put it into the weed that she was rolling to smoke for later. Tina left them there that night. She jumped on her bike and rode to her apartment as fast as she could. She was thanking God the entire ride home. She was so happy that Rhonda told her no. She even thanked her later. The caustic chemicals that were added to crack cocaine made it so addictive. Tina knew that had she taken a hit of that laced joint, she wouldn't have been strong enough to walk away. She could have become an addict and made an ugly crackhead. That is why she tried never to look down on people who fought addictions. It could have easily been her.

God's grace kept Tina from contracting HIV/AIDS over the years of her having careless and unprotected sex/relations. Yes, she had genital herpes, but she felt that she could live with that. The other was a death sentence in her eyes. She felt that He spared her life. She felt that she was still punished, but not to the extent that she could have been.

It was God's grace that kept Christians in Tina's path regardless of where she went in the world. It didn't matter if it was in her personal or career path. It was like He put them there to hold her accountable for her actions

113

and to give her words of encouragement along her journey of life. It was also to keep her on the straight and narrow road whenever she veered left. Tina believed that that was God's way of letting her know that He was always there, even when she didn't feel Him there. He was assuring her that everything was going to be alright.

God's grace broke any ungodly soul ties that Tina may have had. She prayed that He would free her from them because she had so many. His grace also eliminated any generational curses that were upon her and her family. She prayed that He released those as well, so that neither she nor her family would have to suffer in silence. She realized that sex was a powerful thing, and every time someone went into her, voluntarily or involuntarily, there was a soul tie. Even if they did not go into her, but sex was on the premises, in thought or emotion, they were connected to her soul.

It was God's grace that watched over Tina's kids throughout their lives. She knew His grace kept them off the streets and out of jail. His grace also kept her children off drugs. He kept her kids sane and safe through whatever trial and tribulations they encountered. It was by His grace only that her children turned out well and successful.

God's grace kept Tina from drowning in what she believed to be bouts of depression. There were times when she would basically sleep her life away and didn't want to interact with anyone. She would even shut out her family because she didn't want them to see her go through whatever it was that she was going through. Clearly, she didn't know what she was going through, but she didn't want her dismal mood to ruin anyone else's vibe. She felt that it could have been a plethora of things, such as recent lost loved ones, health issues, etc. There were days where she literally walked from the bed to the couch and vice versa. She even went days without taking a shower. She felt that because she wasn't dating and her kids weren't coming over that day that it wasn't a big deal. She pretty much prayed her way through those times and ate everything that she could find in the kitchen.

It was God's grace that gave Tina the strength to finally seek counseling. She was embarrassed at first and didn't think she needed it. Her children encouraged her to go as well. She sought out counseling to confront old memories and feelings that were resurfacing from her past. She thought, it's covered through my job, so why not check it out? Tina let out everything that she had suppressed over the years. She even shed some tears, which she did not do a lot of. She was just not a crier. She didn't want to be viewed as weak because she was indeed a strong black woman. It was a cleansing experience for her. She did the homework that her life coach gave her, which helped her a lot during that process. Tina loved her counseling sessions and was very glad that she had sought counseling.

God's grace comforted her when she lost her loved ones. They were people that she loved dearly, and she wasn't sure how to handle those losses. She prayed, talked to God, hung around family who cared, talked to Raven and wrote poems to deal with her pain. Nothing really took her hurt away. However, these actions made it a little easier to go on with life. She still missed them every day.

It was God's grace that allowed her stepfather and Hospice to take good care of her mom during her final days. Tina's mom was given baths every other day and diaper changes daily. They kept her mom very comfortable with pain management. Her mom had them all waiting on her hand and foot like a true queen. Her mom kept everyone laughing when she could. One day, she went into a peaceful sleep and never woke up again.

It was God's grace that freed Tina from the bondage of her past. He freed her from a damaged and broken heart.

His grace showed her that love could conquer all. Her choice to love instead of hate was her freedom. When she now looked in the mirror she saw a free, grown, imperfect, flawed, independent, God-fearing, beautiful, intelligent, strong, black, virtuous woman who she loved even more. Freedom looked good on her.

God's grace gave Tina continued life. Some years ago, she was diagnosed with a debilitating heart condition. She was scared, wondering if she would have the same fate as her youngest brother, Liam, and her mom. By His grace, with the taking of medications, vitamins, tests, and doctor visits, she made the best out of her life. This was a humbling ordeal. She was blessed and proud to be standing above ground. All the things (degrees, jobs, houses, cars, marriage, etc.) that used to be important to her were no longer important. Because she understood that no one is promised tomorrow and none of those things could be taken with her in death, she chose to enjoy life. She spent most of her time hanging out with her family. When they were happy, so was she. She still had a desire to marry someday.

It was God who healed Tina's brokenness. He forgave her journey to single motherhood. He showered her with the wisdom to pursue her achievements. He provided her with self-love, which was vital to her self-worth. Also, He instilled in her forgiveness, which helped her to forgive. She was so glad that His mercy said no to all that was set out to destroy her! It was His grace that allowed her a renewed sense of life.

"Each time he said, 'My grace is all you need. My power works best in weakness.' So now I am glad to boast about my weaknesses so that the power of Christ can work through me" (New Living Translation, 2 Cor. 12.9).

My Future Husband

Dear My Future Husband,

Just because I am strong, independent, God-fearing, beautiful, and intelligent doesn't mean that I do not need you. I do! Don't be intimidated by me. Get to know me.

Love,

Your Future Wife

www.ingramcontent.com/pod-product-compliance
Lightning Source LLC
Chambersburg PA
CBHW030543130626
46552CB00006B/2396

* 9 7 8 0 6 9 2 1 1 5 4 6 6 *